# MAIN BRIDES
## Against Ochre Pediment
## and Aztec Sky

# MAIN BRIDES

Against Ochre Pediment
and Aztec Sky

## GAIL SCOTT

COACH HOUSE PRESS
TORONTO

© Gail Scott, 1993

FIRST EDITION

*Main Brides, Against Ochre Pediment and Aztec Sky* is a work of fiction. The characters in it have been invented by the author. Any resemblance to people living or dead is purely coincidental.

Published with the assistance of the Canada Council, the Department of Communications, the Ontario Arts Council, and the Ontario Publishing Centre.

Canadian Cataloguing in Publication Data

Scott, Gail
    Main brides, against ochre pediment and aztec sky

ISBN 0-88910-456-5

I. Title.

PS8587.C623M34 1993     C813'.54     C93-093447-4
PR9199.3.S35M34 1993

To my young women friends
whose courage inspires me

*We are the philosophical investigators of*
*the late 20th century. Or only women. Practicing.*

Carla Harryman

**(the sky is what I want)**

Dusk after a June rain. Suddenly some laser rays of setting sun between low clouds cast oval masks on a group of cyclists racing up The Main. Pedalling high-kneed into the narrowing beams aimed almost horizontally along the street. Their bare legs in socks folded at the ankles, flashing past a bar-café.

They flash past (inside, a pair of eyes watches, astonished at how the sun has pressed its oval stamp on knees, foreheads, chins), cycling towards another century. Past the last pickle barrel, over which Mr. Simka bends, a light-beam through his chest; past the artists' building, now transformed into expensive noisy condominiums; past the Portuguese photo store with the bride standing in the window. Her soldier's X'd out. But even if he weren't, she'd be standing there in her white lace with everybody looking: the Main thing in the picture for a single minute of her life. The cyclists pedal fast. Their intense faces like eclipsed moons with only the forward-part lit up.

The eyelids flicker. Across the street, a red-and-white truck marked VIANDE M.A.I.N. has driven up. But, the half-closed eyes have drifted to a park with grass blowing in the wind, and clouds. Sky, growing mauve and pink, and a lace curtain fluttering veil-like in a window. A body lying on its back, legs up, in the green green grass. As if there'd been a crime.

The eyes (green, a woman's) blink again. She lights a cigarette, raising downy neck from crisp, white blouse in a gesture of composure. So her hair, auburn, pulled back a little, her red lips on creamy skin, provide a handsome profile which could be English, French, Portuguese (Lisbon, not the Azores). Her gaze, well-lined in kohl, now on a dark-eyed teenager coming through the door. "Tense," thinks a client, standing by the bar. Noting the empty wine decanter, sweating water-glass, mushed-up bread on the woman's table. "She's been here a while.

"What's she waiting for?"

The client doesn't know what some regular clients know, grouped farther down the counter: she could be here for hours. Sitting quietly in the heat. Smoking cigarettes and watching other people. As if imagining their stories. Possibly, to counter some vague sense of emptiness.

Or else—to forget.

The bar door opens. The woman's gaze shifts, eyes intense with light reflected from the street, to another woman entering, dressed like a mandarin (raised collar, thin shapely mouth). Then back to the teenager: the girl's hand, gripping a café au lait glass; high cheekbones, dark eye-circles; yet young enough to be fresh at the turn of the century.

"If she lasts," adds the woman. Focusing harder on the girl. Taking in, discreetly, the adolescent's various postures, angles.

Suddenly she laughs. Remembering, on the street where the girl grew up, her Greek and Portuguese neighbours called her warmly, jokingly "The Flyer." Because the girl had a habit of dangling dangerously from cornices, or upper apertures—

# Nanette

The girl's hand is wrapped around a napkin wrapped protectively around a tall glass of café au lait. Called a galão in this place. Her clothes, in fashion, though unchanged for the past two years: slim black leather pants, black boots. The straight cut of the dyed black hair making her even paler in the half-light of the bar. Suddenly she laughs with her fine mouth, her small teeth, although not quite the eyes. Trilling almost, as she touches the arm of a blond young man who enters. An indication she has landed on her feet.

Or is it just an act?

The woman blows smoke between her lips (rouged indignant red). Eyes fading again to the park under the crazy leaning garret where she knows the girl, Nanette, grew up. On the garret window of the girl's room, a circle of stained glass: grey, blue, winding to a point where a tiny silver airplane began its high arc beyond the image's edge. Heading towards the sky. The room belonged, before the girl's parents bought the house, to a woman aviator. Who must have loved looking (where the glass remained unstained) beyond the gently swinging grey-brown branches of the park and the high ridge called the mountain to the rhythm of clouds moving daily towards the purpling dusk.

Mornings, waking in that room, the girl felt upside-down. Because her feet, seen from the head of her bed, seemed to touch those clouds. Watching the blue darken behind them left her ecstatic. But also, the indelible impression that time bruises. She swore she'd never let time do that to her. Eating little, and (as if this were an antidote) reading the *Surrealist Manifestoes*. The woman once saw her in the park (thin flowing dress), with a homeopathic treatise that said heroin (in small controlled doses) can keep you young.

Yet—Nanette adored her mother. Walking down the street, holding the older woman's plump sun-marked arm as if her mother were a goddess, she wore a secret smile. Was it for her mother's oddly shaped chignon, rising like a Chinese character above her somewhat heavy form? Or was it merely from some unconscious memory of hugging her mother with her whole body, her whole heart, the way little girls do? "If it weren't for women," she'd say in her pleasant voice, tossing her head sideways, "I don't know what I'd do. My Mom," and (somewhat enigmatically): "feminists."

Then she disappeared. Her light presence, a missing thread in the fabric of the street: the pretty houses that had once vibrated to the dance-music of minor consul parties, later inhabited by immigrants, and recently bought again by the salaried rich, though not the bourgeoisie. While, on nice days, in the park opposite, the playing fields filled up with ever-increasing numbers of soccer teams in brightly coloured uniforms and cleated shoes. Or else military exercises. Only a secret nuns' garden at the bottom of the street was spared the racket.

"Disappeared" is perhaps putting it too strongly.

She was no longer seen looking from behind the fourth-floor window with the stained-glass motif. Watching as the park took on its Gothic shades of night. While below her on the third floor, her brother and sister fought. And on the second, her father and mother communicated the difficulties of family life in English, for they had no other common language: her father being Finnish, her mother, Russian. She was no longer at the window, who, at eight, had moved up to the room in tightly plaited braids she had carefully done herself, to please amid the fighting and the tension. Standing at the window, both terrified and enthralled by the height and solitude, her small head turned sideways.

The absence was hardly noticed (girls naturally leave home). Possibly by a voyeur in the park waiting, in shoes covered with autumn leaves, for her head to be outlined by the blue electric light behind it. And of course, by her mother, who knew vaguely (and didn't like it) where the girl had gone. The woman remembers seeing Nanette later, on the back of a motorcycle plunging like a wild pony down the darkened street that ran between the park and the old wall surrounding the beautiful, secret, perfumed nuns' garden. Urging the driver on with her small hands placed around his waist, her small smile hanging poignantly in the air behind his leather jacket. "Some are born to floating," thinks the woman, a little incongruously.

"And some float late."

She peers across the bar: the girl is scratching her cheeks, scratching her arms. The woman trains her eyes to see if Nanette's pupils are as small as points. Like she thought they were that day outside a Park Avenue rooming-house, where the girl stood, thin, a silhouette of black and blue, her slim legs in calf-length boots. Laughing her head off with a group of punks, some so stiff they could hardly lean forward. One, in a bowler hat, the girl held onto: too good-looking, "feminine," yet mean—. The woman stops. Hating her voyeurism: a greed that parasites lâchement, like society does, on the fragile beauty of what intrigues. Example: her own dependence, always hugging, kissing, that soft delicious cat with thick white hair that could fly from storeys up as if magically indestructible. Yet, in broad daylight, its gaze went blank, and it moved under the dirty wooden steps across the street, recognizing no one.

She stares harder through the bar's dim light. Unable not to notice that the girl looks anxious. Unable not to see her paleness, even more exaggerated than before, as she turns her head constantly towards the door. The girl's blond young friend has gone. She's probably waiting for the other one, the one she saw her with outside the rooming-house. Also, one night he was standing, smiling, all in black, with her in a ladies' washroom the woman stumbled into. The girl turning on all her charm, offering him everything with her mouth, her eyes, her head sideways, pushing her shoulders close to him, begging, smiling even while he answered:

"I haven't got anything, tonight."

The woman orders another carafon.

Her gaze becomes almost somnambulant. Until, like Nanette's in her garret room, it reflects the falling blue beyond the window. A phenomenon (thinks the woman) common only to those whose eyes have the quality of capturing images. That is, dark eyes that see, just by looking up, that if the "line" of reason breaks, a person can do anything. Take in any number of impressions. Visual, aural. Music, songs: *Splish Splash* (someone in a bath). Tires screeching in the night. Graffiti indicating the small solidarities of the century's final decade. Albeit nothing higher than a clarinet playing behind the open door of the piano-bar called G Sharp. (The pain's too much.)

The woman stops. Brushing back her curls to show her profile, aquiline (the kind she likes). Breathing, to settle down a little. Heat plus alcohol are making her ridiculous. Soon she'll be imagining the girl is one of those runaways you read about in *La Presse:*

*Elle fait la fugue. Meets this nice man in the Berri Métro station with whom she spends three days. He gives her $100 and throws her out. Then she meets another, younger, cool. Who dances like a dream on the huge polished floor of Le 13e Ciel. He buys her supper in the middle of the night, under the green glass dome of Le Lux, boul. St-Laurent. Then he takes her to his flat: rugs, pillows, soft colours, music.*

*She can't believe how she's landed on her feet. Three days later he's asking her to sleep with "a friend," then other "friends." It's clear she has to, or lose his love. Not to mention, she has no place to live.*

The woman sits still. Watching the line of Nanette's cheek in profile, looking out the bar window. Suddenly remembering the golden down of the girl's delicious pubescent cheek through dark maple leaves. Nanette, crouched near the tap in the park, legs apart, curled hair, full skirt, ballet slippers, splashing water on the fat body of some baby. The woman sitting next to her (the prerogative of a neighbour). Or, on a bench with her friends. Hands in pockets, shoulders hunched, teasing a flasher who came to sit with them. He'd pull it out, red and swollen. They'd turn their pretty heads, examine it carefully for a minute, then say in chorus: "Oh, is that all?"

Or else, walking with her mother. Rarely with her father, who never spoke, due (the woman thought) to lack of English. Until she heard him discussing soccer with the British coach on the grassy field, later replaced by Astroturf. And saw that Nanette's father knew the language perfectly. Once on Hallowe'en, he opened the oak door with leaded windows of the family's narrow, slightly leaning house. A red nose, flowing hat. Smiling mirthlessly. And gave out apples.

Yes, the girl's okay.

Likely not even waiting for that guy in black——(for the younger generation, the sex has been displaced). The guy, often seen moving alone at night on Park Avenue from bar to bar. Pretending to be important (a roll of bills in his hand). Excessiveness in his charm: exactly what the woman would have wanted in a man 15 years earlier. Once she heard Nanette tell her Greek friend Melina, who wanted, above everything, to go into business: "I read in a book that *women will do anything ... for love, because sex isn't a thing to them.... This is why women can be sexually honest and faithful. This is why women look up to things, are amazed by things.* Isn't that weird? Isn't there more after all this feminism?"

The woman lights a cigarette. Again—the girl (who's pretending not to know her) is scratching her arms. Again the woman strains (despite herself) to catch this note of darkness. Wishing in the damp heat Nanette's friends would come. Not the guy in the hat. But her friend Melina. Or else, the guy whose motorcycle they rode down the street by the secret nuns' garden, like a pony. Nanette (pressing him always faster), clearly wilder than he. Did her mother feel guilty about giving her that high room? The older woman who, out shopping, was sometimes seen watching the street kids standing eagerly on the sidewalk all dressed up (in the shadow of the buildings). Stepping forward, so energetically, so hopefully to solicit, the way young people do on their first job. Knowing that for her daughter, washing dishes in a restaurant or hospital kitchen is likely closer to the truth. But that Nanette would probably only work the minimum 20 weeks before taking out unemployment insurance. Always so secretive, but she could hardly have enough money. Of course she eats nothing. The neighbour, Vera Dubrovsky, saw Nanette in the bar where her son works, smoking cigarettes with an untouched plate in front of her. Hardly a bite of the French fries, salad, rice, chicken. What's she waiting for?

Vera added:

"God keep her safe from dangerous infections."

The woman sips her wine. Still admiring, from a corner of her eye, Nanette's high cheekbones, her leather jacket with the slight rip in it. A sense of style, unique, yet guileless. A sign (she thinks) the girl has understood that to get beyond the difficulty of being self and pleasing others, you have to synthesize the inner and the outer. As in music. As in the notes of that clarinet spilling into the black night from the bar with faded musical notations for steps. Of course, in looking up all the time, the clouds begin to function as palimpsest. In the rhythm, almost, of modern "rap." The small pink cloud backstepping over the grey one. Then forward again into blue. A young black woman with a platinum wavy ponytail sliding down the side. Saying:

"I just want to be myself."

"But what lies behind?" asks the woman in sudden blurred panic. She gets the image of an early-60s television program: children hiding under desks during the Cuban Missile Crisis. "They made voyeurs of us," she thinks, "with their notions of black and white."

To calm herself she takes out her compact. Wanting to tell of the girl like music. Her leaving home, a flight towards love, adventure: like any teenager. The girl's not *her*. Not always sitting poised in some downtown café (like the woman used to do after a day's work in an advertising agency): leather skirt, hooped earrings, Indian shirt. Disappointed she wasn't quite the stunning vision she'd imagined the night before. For the younger generation, the signs are more complex: maybe Nanette's an artist. Didn't her friend Melina, with beautiful golden curls (the budding businesswoman), reply, when someone asked, "How's Nana?":

"Doing what she likes best. Smoking cigarettes and drinking coffee. If we don't shape up, none of us will amount to anything."

The woman snaps her compact shut. The lips she's drawn firmly on her face float smilingly in the cool-hot air to avoid any voyeuristic speculation. Ready now to make the girl's story almost banal. "Fresh unmarked copy," the woman thinks absurdly, her eyes fading to the front steps of Nanette's funny leaning house. (She would, herself, like to be on the point of leaving home again.) Nanette sliding off the steps. Her pointed shoes turning east along the grey-white sidewalk. Never looking back at the high upstairs room she knows her brother with the creepy fingers will immediately move into.

(He can stay there.)

The day is gorgeous. Ten a.m. and Nanette's walking down the street with a Leonard Cohen song ringing in her ears: *They sentenced me to 20 years of boredom / for trying to change the system from within / I'm coming now I'm coming to reward them / first we take Manhattan then we take Berlin.* Music that both buoys her and overwhelms her with its cynicism. Walking light and happy when she sees this guy (she'd met somewhere before) coming towards her in the slush. His clothes, his manner, indicating he can maybe show her something she doesn't know already (about how to keep afloat). Dressed in black and white, a black hat perched jauntily on his head.

His face, pale like hers (under his bowler hat), looks into the shadow of her eyes. He smiles. There's something feminine about the way his full lips, his nose, become involved in this softening of his face. Tossing her head to one side, brushing back the hair she suddenly finds too heavy, she says: "Hello." He hands her his Walkman, playing something about what was done to the sheriff's non-consenting daughter. Laughing, complicitly, as if it were a joke. Seeing the trouble in her eyes, he touches her cheek. Making her suck her fear in, remembering just in time her motto to go through with whatever's offered by *le hazard objectif.* She read this in the *Surrealist Manifestoes.* "What's your facts?" he asks. She laughs and answers (god only knows why):

"Birdland."

He says, possibly overconfident: "I'll take you there." Then, a long afternoon in various cafés (art deco patterns floating on the walls). Later, in his bed, which looked over sheds, flat roofs making an almost bowl-shaped pattern stretching east towards the horizon, he took her layers of skirts off. The sheets pricked, were full of cookie crumbs. He said (joking) he had a sweet tooth as he put his mouth down, gently sniffing, like a puppy, searching out her "honey." Out the window, a cloud moved maddeningly away in the blue sky as she felt the small surge of excitement where she'd hoped for larger. He looked at her, half-ironically. Brushed back his black hair, pleased with himself. She stood up.

She knew she wanted more.

The woman stops, displeased with her narrative.

Outside, a man on crutches is swinging down the street. His head turned up, talking, laughing with his friends, happy despite the useless lower body. A state of mind, the woman thinks, best achieved when obliged by fate to live squarely in the marginal. To maintain this happy state, one has to eat yet avoid being absorbed into any kind of co-opting work—which murders thinking. She recalls (incongruously) the runaway girls lined up in the Berri Métro station. The cute blonde with sunglasses, red lips, felt hat and two-year-old son; the one coming out of the washroom, rolling down her sleeve cheekily, osten-tatiously, so everyone can tell she's had her fix; the girl outside in run-down high-heeled boots, jeans worn thin, leaning into a car to barter. It says in the paper that on the street there's real anti-parent solidarity among the kids. The pimps providing *un encadrement, toutefois sans le côté moralisant, hypocrite de leurs parents souvent abusifs. And certain other pleasures. Which help the girls forget that by a curious phenomenon of psychological repression, they actually blame themselves for their lack of self-respect.*

But—Nanette has spirit.

The woman sips her wine. Wishing the girl's friends would come. Maybe her friend Melina, who wants to go into business. Already making lists with her stubby fin-gers, painted dramatic red. Melina, who was the single person to see through her. She'd say to Nanette's sister:

"I can't get her down from that tower. She just stands up there staring at the clouds." Secretly, she didn't blame her: going into Nanette's house gave her the creeps. So dark behind the crooked oak door (her own was blue and white and vined). And the way Nanette's mother used to always sit down on a chair before going out the door. In her heavy coat, for luck, or something.

Across the bar, the girl (even whiter than before) is pushing aside her café au lait as if it's poison to her. Lighting a cigarette. Not that she's anorexic. Just anxious, like any normal person, because her friends are late. Melina, and the guy in black (it's hard to exclude him). He, too, lighting a cigarette as he moves along the sidewalk. Oh, he's stopped. He's leaning against a wall cajoling Melina. No. M.'s against the wall and he's leaning over her, joking. Menacing. Nanette laughs self-consciously. But under the white skin, the high cheekbones, the dark-rimmed eyes, her jaw is set in determination to experience any sensation life brings her. The value of a mask being that of an anchor to the surface. This she knew already when, in pigtails, she moved up to her high room: that everybody had a mask, even if they weren't "dressed up." That's why, when they offered her the rabbit costume on Hallowe'en, she said: "Amelia Earhart or I'm not going."

Then she hugged her mother with her whole heart: the older woman in a spotless cotton skirt. Which went up in the back slightly when she leaned over the window at night waiting for her daughter to come home (across the park). Never speaking her concern. Nanette did the same, all her subterfuges having the one goal of reassuring those around her she was having the perfect adolescence. So she could be left alone in her high room. Even after that incident in the park (very minor). Saying nothing. Only taking her mother's arm and asking her: "Could I have a new full skirt? I want to go to a party and dance my heart out." Melina said after: "I've never seen Nanette so active."

The woman wants a cup of coffee. She wants to drive out the tiredness of the century. To be the age of the girl. She looks at the girl's trim back in trendy jacket as Nanette steps neatly towards the counter. A nice walk, casual, yet determined. Oh. She's going to phone. Never (thinks the woman, sipping a little more) is the fresh air of spring so invigorating as at the time of stepping free. Rejecting what protects you. Walking headily down the street. Your pointed shoes in fine leather picking out the dry spots on the sidewalk. Between the patches of quickly melting slush.

The girl turned east. Towards the French sector rather than the English. In search of what? Maybe a room that looked out on factory buildings. On dark, flat squares of gravel covering lower roofs, instead of on parks, people. Plus a little sky. Nanette, in her life, requiring only the slimmest thread of continuity: a windowful of clouds. Having decided not even to finish school. Where, during the emptiness of those classes, she'd read André Breton, who said he was interested exclusively in what was *at the mercy of chance*. Handing in the same term paper to every teacher. The only one she wrote. Until, feeling slightly weird, she decided to rewrite and update a little. The teacher said: "I suspect you of plagiarizing." "You wouldn't believe," the girl answered, "that I plagiarized myself."

Then she "disappeared."

"In search of what?"

The woman runs a finger along her collar. There's an error in the portrait. She glances over (trying to make eye contact). But the girl (with the same ironic smile as when she used to sit in the park, her delicious gold-flecked cheeks bent over some book like *Nadja*), is beckoning to the waitress. The one with black hair and boots, twirling past the tables. Nanette, reaching for her skirt. Cocking her head up in mock patience (the black eye-circles making her even more attractive). Waiting for her to stop: in her high sweet voice, some indistinguishable question, rising above the racket of the bar.

"In search of what?" the woman repeats, tipping her empty carafon (a drop of sweat falling between her breasts). She hates this eternal restlessness of the body. At the girl's age, it would hit her at the end of yet another boring day of work. Or else, a love affair. She'd pack her bags and move. Or set out on a trip. With everybody's words ringing in her ears. "You're going hitchhiking in North Africa, you must be crazy." What'd she care what happened? By the time she got to the yellow ferry-depot at Algeciras, she was feeling vaguely better. The port town had dusty streets and thick, black coffee in its little, dark cafés. Unfortunately, the love she found in a dusty souk, a Nordic hippie selling bicycles in Casablanca, turned sour. Dragging herself beside him, along desert roads, through palm-swept oases, she promised if things weren't better by the time they got to Egypt, she'd walk into the soup-warm sea. Until it closed over her.

But Nanette is more complex.

Melina would get the narrative better. Melina, who once asked Nanette's mother straight out why she was always sitting down in that big coat, before opening up the door (Nanette didn't know). Melina reproached her friend for her lack of initiative. But because she loved her, even if she knew better, she still wanted Nanette to some-day go into business with her.

"C'mon, don't you want a piece of the action?"

Nanette just smiled, causing Melina a pang of envy. Some people got what they wanted without even trying. She didn't mean that guy. His black eyes leaning over her the other day. A girl could go on a good trip easy with him—. But Nana was kidding herself if she thought she could handle the situation. Already she was looking like she was using herself up. They wouldn't be calling her a "classic beauty" for long. Melina thought this almost tri-umphantly. For it was hard to talk herself out of the fact that Nana had some quality that she, shorter, stockier, didn't. Although the category of "classic beauty" Melina found stupid: in Greece, where they should know what "classic" meant, her anorexic friend wouldn't add up. Still, she grew furious when someone said:

"Nana's nothing special.

"And if she doesn't watch out she's going to get addicted."

"What, addicted?" said Melina. "To the clouds, maybe."

The woman smiles. Sitting straighter (to emphasize the small waistband of her dark slim skirt). Approving the rectification to the portrait. Leaving home, a girl can do anything. She has to believe this in order to move forward. Opening the door in her quick gentle way. Walking down the street. To her right (west) the fake Gothic castle in the pink light on the side of the hill they call the mountain. Turning east (left), on the grey-white sidewalk, towards her small account at the Royal Bank. Feeling the imprint on her of everything around: wallposters, traffic music, car exhaust, the earth infused with melting snow. Knowing she wanted more. More than anyone in her family, or Melina, or anyone that she knew. Then she hesitates.

In the hot bar, the woman asks for wine. Her glance grazing the girl. Who's speaking rapidly. Grabbing the arm of the waitress beautiful as a diva, to make her stop spinning. Then the girl's sweet treble, now (due to a pause in the music) audible above the cacophony.

"My friend died."

The music starts again. The woman (wanting wine) tries to think what happens next in the narrative: Nanette's pointed shoes splashing through the craters in the greywhite sidewalk. She turns left again, down rue Maguire. An old post office. A few flat red houses before the railway tracks. She climbs up some steps. Throws a door open (god knows how she found this place). Immediately enchanted by the huge square window with a view of tall chimneys and gently tinctured sky. Instead of the fake prettiness of residential neighbourhoods. The desire to be alone. The space of being anything you want opening up before you. Also, it was great not having to daily contemplate her mother's worried face.

"He smashed his motorbike!" (the girl's high voice verging on hysterical).

The woman also asks for water. Wondering why the older often try to cut the euphoria of the younger. Such as her jealousy of the flying ways of that soft, delicious cat. She wanted to squeeze it sometimes. Or the girl's mother. Her spotless cotton skirt raised behind, as she looked furtively into the darkness of the park. Unable to calculate whether it was really later than it should have been. Regretting how she'd ignored the child when younger. With the problems of getting adjusted to the new country: all that work. (And the marriage was an error: that Finn never spoke.) Causing them to distance. The girl, getting up that last day in her mother's house (not long after the minor incident in the park). Her feet on the cold floor headed down the stairs for a bath in camomile. A ritual of cleansing. Remembering as she did that André Breton started out from *L'Hôtel des Grands Hommes* to discover what chance could bring.

This made her feel weird.

The girl's voice (another pause in the music): "I have to get out of here. I had $3,000—now it's all gone."

It's then the woman's thoughts slip even farther to where she didn't want them to: Nanette in her rented room. Lying watching the ruffled pink of sunset. On the wall: a picture of a tree-trunk with a boy's face on it. On her crumpled bedspread, a pen and paper. Soon she'll do some automatic writing. As soon as she's in the mood. Right now, she's waiting for the moment to get up and cross the floor. Covering the small space between the large bed (now turned towards the huge empty space beyond the window) and the dresser. She always takes her time, to prove that she can wait. She opens the small square of plastic on the dresser's painted black top. Dusts off a space and makes a careful line. The woman watching greedily. Nanette's eyes close (having completed her little ritual). In a minute she'll step through the window to the roof.

Again the woman stops herself, emptying her glass. (Knowing she's projecting.)

She sits very still. Eyes neutral (as if repressing something). Noticing only how the smoke hangs horizontal in the light-rays of the bar. A space of time passes. Suddenly a commotion at the door. A drunk, breaking a bottle, lunging at the crotch of another.

Then, in the silence that always follows clatter, the girl's high voice once more:

"I'm sick of this gig."

The woman steals a look: Nanette talking not to the waitress, but to a baby-faced guy with a camera. Not the one with the bowler hat. This one soft, liberal-looking (a slight tightness of the mouth).

"You want to get out, you git," he says, laughing. "You're a free woman." He stands there waiting. Nanette gets up and goes to the washroom.

There follows an interminable riff of heavy-metal music.

The woman makes an effort: the guy could be a video artist—

But they're getting up to go. Nanette, hair now attached in wings atop her head; vaguely Slavic eyes looking oriental with the additional strokes of makeup; face white as a mask; lips cherry red; black décolleté leotard under her leather jacket. Walking by the woman's table, she sticks out her tongue.

**(the sky is what I want)**

The woman (her name is Lydia) stares out the window.

Occasional clients might confuse her with a Portuguese woman, slightly older. Who comes in every day, keys twirling, waiting for her lover. Elegant in a European way. Dressed in crisp white blouse, slim skirt, like Lydia. Who (at 39) is already a little out of fashion. Compared to the students parading down the sidewalk: black tights, loose tops, brightly coloured crushed hats. "Carnivalesque," she thinks, squinting at the sunset into which the cyclists have ridden. Clouds and sky paling behind the fake pointed pediment rising like an ochre Aztec pyramid over the façade across the street. Making her feel empty, guilty. The way you do after passionately claiming love from someone you never wanted. Or after ... voyeurism.

She lights a cigarette.

Regular clients know her better. Probably regard her as less mysterious. (Albeit, with high cheekbones under matte skin, still incredibly attractive.) Sitting quietly at her table, reflecting on the signs of the epoch. Her hair is shiny. Her fingernails are red. She just feels like this because the air is full of business (cette fois, in French). Although fashion, that harbinger of the future, is swinging back to the craziness she likes. Precisely at the moment when she has corrected from 70s jeans and shirt in a more conservative direction. The best thing is to wait it out. *Do nothing*. Appearance being, naturally, a trope for something else. Dance to a little Latin music: if only they would play that *mambo* tape she likes.

She sips a little wine. Smiling at the thought of *Lydia Waiting*. Not for love (as the regular clients think), but for History. For the greedy decade to give way to lust and revolution. Although she'll keep this look in case she gets a job. Adding maybe a touch of boldness to blend in with the success-oriented women of The Main. Who look more European than North American in their short black dresses, little hats, bright blouses, bows, seamed stockings, cupid mouths. In this heat, Lydia only hates the stockings. For a minute she wishes she were the fasting woman she was in the park this morning. With that clean new-baby feeling you get after not eating for a while. Watching the sudden flash of fuchsia as the sun rises. Splashing the bellies of white gulls as they soar towards the morning sky above the mountain. And the metal band of geometric patterns trimming the edge of a flat-roofed building across the street. Maybe cabalist. She knew she could decipher them. She could do anything she wanted (then, she saw that shadow on the grass).

Lydia lights a cigarette. Feeling a quickening in her some call anger. She glances at the pale blue stretch outside the window. In case the sky is getting closer to that point of emptiness, forcing a terrifying lucidity. Her gaze then fixing meditatively on the greyness of the sidewalk. On the people going back and forth, almost hypnotically, beyond the glass. Creating a state of somnambulism preferable to drunkenness (she should slow down a little). In which there's incredible ease of movement regarding all whims unconnected to signs of what's-to-be-forgotten.

Still, she sips some more.

The door opens. In comes that Portuguese woman who's dressed as conservatively as she. But with very full lips. A brown chignon like the female lead in Cocteau's *Orpheus*. She comes in every day, smoking steadily, twirling her keys, having driven in from the suburbs. Then sits or telephones, waiting for her lover, a square older guy in black leather and motorcycle cap. They talk. Play games on scraps of paper. "A-é-r-i-e-n," says the woman, learning French. Opening her mouth, sticking the tongue out as if to pronounce the sounds as she writes them. Albeit in pure sexual provocation. "As in poste aérienne," says the man impatiently, head averted, looking out the window. Always cranky. They sit there for hours, the sexual tension mounting.

Lydia finds such delays infinitely aesthetic. Waiting also opens up the space of melancholy. Which she sometimes cultivates in revolt against certain positivist ideas. Positive can be shallow. She imagines herself the woman who, in the Cocteau film, goes to meet the devil. Drinking bica in a café in Lisbon. Dunking in one of those sweet little rice-flour cakes they have over there. Outside, prostitutes, but no connection. The stone square full of morning strollers. The street, cobblestone, leading down to a high arch through which the waves shine. All those beautiful girls with red lips, jaunty clothes and smooth white skin coming in for breakfast before going to the office. Their hands! "Oh look, autocar armé," says the woman, happy. To her square and cranky lover. Offering him with her eyes the khaki bus of soldiers driving up The Main. "God," thinks Lydia, "this woman must be left over from the Salazar regime in Portugal."

Anyone can make an error.

She glances down the street. To where Mr. Simka's closing up his shop. The lightbeam that earlier pierced his chest now diffused to a blue-grey reflection on his window, duffed with clouds. In the story of Nanette, also, only a windowful of clouds supplied the slimmest inner thread of continuity. Until something (voyeuristic) burned the movement of the surface. Lydia's kohl-rimmed eyes move restlessly about. "At least," she thinks, "my search for subjects makes the newer clients consider me an artist." As for the older clients (who find her less intriguing than she is) they're seen in turn as inadequate by her. The delegates of failure: Ralph, the drunken sailor from Cape Breton; the video addict, a failed writer; Teresa, the speeded-up waitress (the one who was talking to Nanette).

Lydia tolerates them. Liking familiarity at a distance. What she really wants is "brides." Women on the roof. So the skyline (around the pediments) won't be empty at this moment of the day. When the light turns pale and flushes. When the great gap opens up before the night: manufacturing alcoholics.

"Brides," she repeats, smiling. Because, for a single moment, the Main thing in the picture. Needing only to shake the frame a little to reveal (within their eyes) *that livid sky where hurricane is born.*

(It's true she's drunk too much.)

In the background, the *mambo* tape starts playing.

A woman (in a cheap cotton shirt with little fishes printed on it) gets up and steps out beside her table. Tentatively to the beat. There's a strain at the corner of her eyes. Lydia's never before seen someone who, when they smiled with their mouth, smiled with their eyes less.

Her gaze quickly (discreetly) seeks another source of inspiration. Example: the woman near the phone, with freckles, short dark curls. Licking her lips with enormous pleasure as she sips the amber beer in her glass. A woman capable of enjoying every minute. Even if her eyes are darkly circled. Even if she gets up often (obsessively) to dial. Staring incredulously yet ironically into the receiver when there's no answer at the other end. An ever-increasing frown stamped on her brow.

Lydia silently admonishes the woman. Neutrality of expression prevents a face from prematurely aging. Still, the woman has spirit. Possibly a traveller. Maybe a little dated in her dress: pink cotton V-neck summer shirt worn more with the sloppiness of the 70s than with the artifice that marks the 90s nonchalance in fashion (i.e., more like herself than Nanette). Possibly from a smaller city. At least she pays care to the detail of her nails, the perfection of her skin, the spring in her hair.

Sitting erect in her crisp white blouse, Lydia notes that the deep frown of the woman with the curls disappears immediately as she drinks her beer again. The half-smiling curve of her pink lips growing ever more deliciously ironic. Probably a train-traveller. Doing the run between Montréal and Moncton. Or Kingston/Halifax.

"Halifax," thinks Lydia.

## Main Bride Remembers Halifax

She's in a telephone booth in Kingston. A greystone motel like a fort or prison. And at last she's talking to the one she loves. He's on the telephone in some stone garrison, saying: "Great, let's get together. I'll call later to confirm a time." Smiling, she hangs up. Remembering all the duties of a young officer. She thinks of them in terms of clothes. Rigorously organized into red tunic and pillbox hat for gala dress; otherwise the navy tunic (albeit same pants and hat); probably jogging pants or those regulation shorts for lounging around the cadets' quarters with the guys. Hair on legs lolling restlessly on beds, with socks: white; or navy if the lazy cadet has not completely changed from street wear. An officer-in-training (and gentleman) must be perfect. Must have the regulation kind of condoms stashed safely in his mess kit.

She asked him once: "Don't you think all this organization kind of stifles the imagination?"

He answered, leaning his head, at the time wearing the pillbox, to one side, his lisp audible only when talking to her fondly: "Our commandant says, the more rigorous the structure, the more imagination is required to operate brilliantly within it."

She sits on the edge of the green bed in the motel room in Kingston. Amusing herself by noting these thoughts in a diary. The brown waters of Lake Ontario lap outside her window. (What's she doing in this town anyway?) Waiting for the dry little man with the hornrimmed pince-nez, a university drop-out, to notify her she's received a phone call. Time goes by with greater and greater anguish. She daren't go to eat for fear of missing him. Finally it's dark. The grey day sinking into night marking a terrifying point in her personality she doesn't want to think about.

She gets up. Feeling a little guilty, stupid, she goes into the hall to try for one last telephone communication. The line cracks. Over the cracked line she asks if this is him. The voice says Cadet Jack or John Christian, soon to be Lieutenant. It says the earlier possibility of an encounter seems to have faded. At least for tomorrow and tomorrow and tomorrow. She hasn't got the money to stay until after that. She feels the potential softness of his cheek fleeting from her grasp. There is this terrible static on the line. She tries to tell him it's just fine, in order for him not to feel pressured. At the same time trying to find out if there isn't some tiny opening in his schedule. Even if it's not the evening over drinks and dinner in a candle-lit restaurant made of stone dating from the early 1800s. She realizes it might be someone else on the line. Slowly she hangs up. And walks towards the exit.

Outside the motel front, a dusty road. Passing a little church made of very old stones. Very New England Puritan in design, with iron netting over broken stained-glass windows. The road narrows in the dim grey, almost silver evening. A single raindrop making a lace pattern in the dust. She takes a step, slim, long-legged in her dark pants and leather boots. As if she's stepping towards another era. Her forgotten hunger, her fatigue still masked by nerves fed with endless cigarettes, plus the silver shadowed light (especially, the light) making her as weightless as a ghost. But she's too exhausted to make any big decisions now. Besides it's going to rain. Back on the green bedspread she stares at the nearly black water beyond her window. Taking out her diary she notes a dream:

*I'm crossing Peggy's Cove (near Halifax where I grew up) in a boat. Watching the long curve of the green bay and the bluegrey waves on which the boat goes carefully up and down. Feeling worried that the boat won't get there fast enough. The high arc of its tiny bow hardly seeming to advance over the greying expanse of water in the dimming light that divides us from the shore. But at last we get there and I ask: "Where's John C.?" His family, defiant but sympathetic, says: "You missed him," from where they're sitting on a green patterned sofa against dark-blue patterned wallpaper. The mother further clashes because in a flowered housedress.*

This image troubles her. She looks between the Kingston motel curtains at the black lapping water outside her window. Sure that her young officer's family had more "class." That they were members of the yacht club and had good real-estate on the Northwest Arm in Halifax. That they served every different kind of alcohol in the proper kind of glass. Outside their house curled a gravel road through wooded properties where, growing up, he pretended to be an Indian. After which the road emerged in a modest commercial district, then climbed past a graduated row of clapboard houses. Where (although they barely met until she went to university in Kingston) she grew up, the only daughter of a sea-captain father and an ordinary mother. When her father went to sea, he'd walk down the hill on the gravel road between the trees. Turn and wave, walk to the bottom of the street and turn and wave again. They were watching from the kitchen window. Then, her dark curls would be bent over the kitchen table, colouring, drinking chocolate. Perfect peace.

At night, between the sheets, the windows open on the quiet street, masturbation came easily. A touch, a whoosh, and that was it: a happy adolescence. It's true, the pregnancy interrupted her, and her mother's smooth domestic surface. Luckily, they were able to hide it from her father, gone to sea at the crucial moment (the last six months). He came home to find her pale, bedridden, fluish. That was all. As her mother said: "Think nothing more of it." She didn't—until seeing the given-up baby's father on a train going east. Walking down the aisle. As he held the seats for ballast, she took in his short waist, his brief, well-built legs, especially the long black hair typical of the rebels in that family.

Her young officer was of an entirely different type. Slightly British accent. Long-legged, big, almost feminine hips, fortunately balanced by the padded shoulders of his uniforms. It was when she brought this "fiancé" home from university that her father ventured an opinion about her sexual appetite. Disgust. After he surprised them in the kitchen, kissing. Kissing, kissing: she could have literally drunk from her young officer's lips. What is the colour of an obsession? Red. But to think it could show up in a red tunic in east-end Montréal, where she found herself after their estrangement, was ridiculous. Québécois were known for their hate of garrisons. Yet she looked for that red jacket everywhere she went. Notably in bars around her flat— a third-floor walk-up in a funny painted building looking over an empty parking lot. It was a weird coincidence that she shared a common entrance with some members of a subversive environmental group. Unfortunately, her small obsession showed. Her neighbours, although they liked her, quickly began to indicate suspicion of her many different lives. "Women, like cats, have nine," she answered them respectfully. For she admired their understanding of how the system makes us crazy.

"Good thing I didn't find him, too."

She suddenly thinks this, sitting bolt upright on the green bedspread of the motel room in Kingston (it's some years later—does she even look the same?). Because it suddenly occurs to her he might have been functioning as an undercover agent. Trying to find out her friends. Using his deceivingly ingratiating ways, his handsome blondness, to get to all the women. So what's she doing in this town anyway? Just a convenient milk-stop for the train. Besides, he wasn't what her friends the anarchist environmentalists presumed. Belonging as he did to a new liberal tendency in the military. Impassioned with poetry, music—like a 19th-century hero. He'd only joined the navy to get to university. She now remembers clearly: his family didn't really live on the Arm. That was another wealthier branch headed by his uncle, le Général Le Flô. Who used to say, sitting on the patterned sofa:

"I can't wait for the next war."

On the bedspread of her motel room in Kingston, she returns to the colour of her obsession. An image is like a door. She thinks this, absent-mindedly, unbuttoning her burgundy-red shirt to reveal the pink cotton top; one of the many layers of clothing of a woman who travels light. Suitcase bulging mostly with accessories capable of transforming a simple outfit into a multitude of images. Stepping forward carefully. Although the desire to please may be mostly on the surface.

Speaking of red, maybe her young officer got turned off that day riding up to Red Lake. They were together again after a long separation. She so happy, she sang out of tune all the way. Having been to the yacht club, courtesy, precisely, of his uncle, le Général Le Flô. She in a homemade brown dress with a drawstring at the waist. First they'd had a yacht-ride. Then sat on the upper gallery drinking gin and watching the waves gently lap the yachts anchored in the harbour. A single gull was rising in the flawless blue sky. When looking down, her young officer suddenly saw two girls he "knew from school now going to a smart New England university." And disappeared for quite a while. She focused on the bottom of her glass until something positive came up. His tiptoeing that morning into the room where she was sleeping at his mother's place. Blue chintz curtains blowing in the sea air. She was wearing short chintzy blue pyjamas, too. And he came tiptoeing in, his regulation condom already stuck on his hard red prick. Saying not to worry, his mother wouldn't notice.

At breakfast his mother said: "My girl, you're too conciliatory."

Outside the Kingston motel window, the lake's as black as ink. But—what's happening to the earth depends on one's angle of perception. Same with what's happening in relationships. His and her problem likely was they could never get together for any length of time: his garrison kept moving. Halifax, Montréal, back to Kingston. Even a few years later, she sometimes tried to follow. Where she got her money was unclear, but she could still afford the trains. Constantly on the move like others, richer, in Toyotas, planes. Plying minor trades to avoid the emptiness of this part of the century. (She never took the bus.)

In fact, this whole story might be more appropriate on a train. Young officers were all over the place in those days. Post-Vietnam, when men still openly dreamed of war. Their cocky voices shouting out in garrison mess-halls: "*Latin America next*" (History proved them wrong: it was the Mohawks and Iraq). Red and blue tunics running between garrisons, that is, bases. Young women leaving seasonal cotillions, heading east to Montréal, west to Toronto. In railway cars put on special, with such round and steamy sides, it was rumoured they might, before refurbishing, have served as cattle-cars.

No, garrisons. The 19th century died hard in Canada. It died in 1970.

Now it's 1975. Maybe 1980 (give or take a decade). What's she doing in this town anyway? She gets up from the green bedspread. Outside the motel window, black waves lapping under dark clouds. Swollen with the night and 100 years of industrial revolution. A few years back, they were still having real winters. She remembers going to Montréal during one, after a Christmas ball (prior to their estrangement, although she'd already left the Kingston university to "job hunt" in larger cities).

Anyway, winter on the train: still in her ballgown. It was cold and snowing. The cattle-car had red velvet seats and was full of elementary-school teachers striving to improve their possibilities. He (her young officer) stood outside in the snow. So involved with drinking from his whiskey bottle, then joking with the guys, he didn't even properly wave goodbye to her little triangular face watching through the steamy window. Her brown eyes smiled bravely at the cadet in the seat opposite who also happened to be travelling to her destination. They raised their glasses. Unfortunately, she was unable to transfer her affections.

Thank god the train was moving.

Her pale reflection in the window reminded her of something. Pulling out her lipstick, she changed her image from the natural look obligatory for the "fiancée" of Cadet Jack or John Christian soon to be Lieutenant. To a cosmo-politan 40s-style woman. By simply darkening the mouth in a firm and generous stroke of red red lipstick. So that even the pink shirred strapless evening gown she wore was transformed from demure to worldly. There she was: maybe not so marriageable. But bold, confident of her sexuality to the point of being devastating. A woman who could do anything with a man because so distanced from the act she was putting on.

Stretching out her feet on the motel bed in Kingston (still with her boots on), she smiles at the image. Suddenly remembering this persona as a young girl. By a dusty baseball diamond back in Halifax. When the dusks in larger villages and smaller cities still gave the illusion there was space to become anything you wanted. Standing there, allegedly to watch the boys play, she was in reality sizing up the girls. Overweight Ella B., whose father openly slept with other women, including Ella's friends. Beautiful (but bitchy) Carmel, whose old man had a temper. La tristesse of Sandra M., whose dad had other ways of keeping daughters down. Compared to them, she, Adèle (named by her romantic poetry-loving mother after a French poet's daughter), felt very fortunate in terms of family consequences: her boat-captain father was mostly absent. Something told her to ensure this situation persisted regarding male encounters. Keeping up a distance by putting on an act. Right there and then she determined to speak only with a deep throaty voice: a means used by courtesans in French and Russian novels.

She gets off the bed of her motel room in Kingston. Attractive in the silver-grey television light in jeans over cowboy-style boots, very slim belted waist, burgundy-red shirt. Briefly leaving the room to order pizza. She eats the smallest slice, then lights a cigarette while writing in her diary: *Ce qui fait déraper une femme, ce n'est pas le sexe. Mais la bouche du père.* A dried-apple mouth which trembled while he bathed her. Or held some argument on politics or sea travel at the kitchen table. She had in common with her namesake, Adèle H., that her diary, while she lived at home, quoted her father frequently. At the encouragement of her mother, who had married him reluctantly. And was trying to make him feel important, "preserving certain phrases" so he wouldn't get suspicious and give up his sea trips. (He had a rather small boat.) She, Adèle, the appointed scribe, sat down at the table, opening her notebook. Just as her father said to Victor-Jean, the student working for him summers: "I am for both democracy and war. This is possible, since I believe in God."

"Maman, est-ce que je peux avoir mes oeufs?"

"Écris, tu auras tes oeufs plus tard."

What makes these things come back all of a sudden? A memory of her shiny lower torso. The kitchen painted yellow. Her mother stationed, like the Queen of Hearts, behind her teapot. Not pleased with Adèle's "fiancé," Jack or John Christian. Because the older woman had spent years trying to pawn her daughter off on Victor-Jean, who, while eating plaice, would try proving to her father that a democrat is of necessity anti-royalist. Adèle hated the insecurity of his presentation: always piling up the proof, opening his soul and speaking loudly. Contrary to her mother, who said repeatedly: "He has no secrets: he'll provide you with stability." Adèle preferred her "fiancé" Jack or John Christian's cooler attitude. Admitting he knew *dick* about politics: his fields of expertise being sports, food, love. He'd say this in his charming, slightly lisping voice, accompanied by a sideways glance of his blue eyes, while grasping one of her pretty curls. Which he then bent over reverently.

The voice suddenly lost its lisp, had an edge of hard flint that day, driving up to the brick Red Lake. When he said coldly: "Stop singing. You've been out of tune all the way." In the bright sunlight, the edge of flint blinded. Of course, she didn't take it passively. Always trying to turn a disadvantage, she was kissing, kissing him in the Red Lake. Pulling back the crotch of her dark bathing suit, so he would do it to her right there in the water. Forgetting (in the process of trying to improve her possibilities) to act detached. This was her fundamental error.

But this story is more appropriate on a train. Trains enjambing time. Full of women, happy, laughing at their little victories, in the decades that followed up the various wars of the century. Although—staring out at him standing on the dark, disappearing platform after the Christmas ball—her eyes got that flinty feeling. Kind of terrifying. Until she realized she just had to turn from looking, her hand digging for the red red lipstick in the beaded evening bag. Boldly made-up, she raised her glass again (in the game way that made everybody like her) at the cadet across the aisle. Distraught as she was, she liked this feeling of detachment. Stepping off the train, wildly attractive with excitement and with anguish, she saw her neighbours, les Dinosaures Anarchistes, in the Café de la Gare. Distributing tracts calling for workers to take forced

control of public railways, before the privatizing government dismantled them completely. *"For the sake of air!"*
the English tract said. She stood and watched. Shivering
in her pink ballgown and rabbit-fur jacket, given the
dampness of the station. Bertrand-de-Matane looked up,
disappointed. "Revolutionaries," he said, "should move in
every level of society for information purposes. But I think
you're overdoing it." He added (eyeing her rabbit jacket
with disgust) that the military college, with its balls and
formalities designed to make boys from ordinary families
feel superior, was really 19th century. Instituted for purposes of imperialist expansion.

Later to keep minorities in hand.

If only she could get the 19th century and 20th
together before the 21st arrives. These are her thoughts as
she half-rises to go to the cigarette machine in the motel
hall in Kingston. Not that time matters a thing to her.
She's a woman entirely without ambition. Preferring
movement, texture, light to pompous speeches regulated
by ticking clocks in university classrooms. Lying back (for
just another minute) on the green bedspread, this time-
lessness enables her to imagine any future to fill the empty
present. Example: going to another city and starting over.
Or, giving in to her desire to rent a room in Halifax,
where her young soon to be Lieutenant Jack or John
Christian's garrison is getting posted. Looking at the
Kingston motel's simulated pine-covered walls, she wonders why after that last Christmas Ball back in, she forgets
what year—he never called again. Possibly due to all her
travelling (an address in every province to beat the welfare

system): Montréal and Halifax, sometimes back to Kingston. The train quickly became her favourite mode of transportation. She loves the clacking, clacking. The landscape fleeting outside the windows. The sense of expectation when the conductor says:

"Mesdames, messieurs, nous arrivons à Montréal.

"Watch your step."

(In the bar in Montréal, Lydia grasps her glass.)

Meanwhile what to do in a motel room in Kingston? Not turn the television on again because it makes her feel alienated. Smoke another cigarette to mask that faint but nagging hunger? She gets off the bed. Outside the window, the observation tower of the Kingston penitentiary casts a beam of light on the black water. She could go for a walk. Stepping forward, outlined by the silvery moon. Down that long road with its strange light along the dark edges of the 19th-century buildings. Nineteenth century. There's that phrase again, although it's 1975, maybe much later. Is repetition the colour of an obsession? Nineteenth-century women (depending on their class) travelled all over the place wearing loose buns, wrapped in steamer rugs, legitimately following young officers. In the 20th century, these things began to change. She passes her hand over her diaphragm in a gesture of closing up the wound: in Halifax, her young officer would probably accept to come over. Especially if she appealed to him coolly, in a letter, as a friend trying to get re-established in the city. Yes, this non-threatening approach should work: he's likely still suffering from rejection because she took off so quickly (to avoid winter

examinations) from Kingston, where he was garrisoned at
the time. Although returning, as she'd promised, for the
Christmas Cotillion Ball. Her hand moves to her cunt.
Head averted (to avoid a terrifying point in her personality
she doesn't want to think about).

What makes these things come back? Her mother
behind her teapot, complaining of inconvenience. Little
lying narratives about her daughter's rootlessness. "My
girl, you're all over the place. You'll get some disease."
Adèle shut her out, thinking about a shiny house she saw
in a dream (oddly *Dead Red Brick*, her dream title said):
the same house she used to see while driving Sundays
with her parents outside Halifax. "—from man to man as
if you didn't care," her mother finished up. Adèle replied:
"Not really."

There's nothing like having sex with someone you
really want.

A shiny point of light.

She lies back again, spreadeagled on the bed. In the
same pink top (making her look vulnerable), the same smile
half-happy, half-sad, as when observed by Lydia in the bar
in Montréal. Trying for one more telephone communication. Before sitting down and ordering yet another Brador.

On the bed in the motel room in Kingston, the
smile fades completely. Because thinking (not too much)
of her desire for the young officer. But, also of her desire
to keep moving, always beautiful, a heroine who's made an
art of living in a completely contemporary way. Lacking
money, but the worst part about this otherwise very
intriguing life is lacking a pair of warm and tender arms.

*Oof,* she can currently do without. As for the future—she raises herself slightly, thinking the motel-room door handle's turning. Maybe she's got a call. She waits patiently for something to break the silence. Nothing but a slight lifting of a curtain because the window doesn't fit. The door handle, an optical illusion.

Anyway, in Halifax they'll finally get to talk. He in his red tunic, having been to some dress affair first. He does look better in it than in the blue, since it draws attention from his rather large hips. He comes in, polite, his head inclining gracefully towards the old couple: her landlords. His swagger stick at his knee, impressing them with his manners. (In the manner of her namesake Adèle H., the 19th-century French poet's daughter) she's told them they're engaged. The old folks, who are egotistical like most old people (because empty power vessels), talk too much and refuse to leave the room. Just sit there pouring tea and trying to ask, albeit discreetly, when he's coming back and when the wedding is. Before she can figure out a tactic, he suddenly jumps up, stands very straight in his military way, and says he has some duty. She can't believe it. She hasn't been alone with him long enough even to put her pale, slightly rouged cheek against his naturally pink and white one. To hold him, kiss him (although she'd primed herself to take it easy, not to scare him).

This whole story would definitely be more appropriate on a train. She must get up and pack. Time passes on a train, unlike in waiting, waiting in some musty-smelling rooming-house with flowered wallpaper in Halifax. Explaining to that old couple, while staring honestly at them from behind her wire glasses (of all her images, the well-scrubbed intellectual was the one she liked the least), that her "fiancé" hadn't come because his commandant, the bastard (this latter implied rather than said), was bigger on duty than on giving passes to let his men leave the base.

True, he would drop in at Christmas. Bringing her a present from his aunt, Mme. le Général Le Flô, who, he says, is "worried." Yeah, thinks Adèle (unable to avoid a touch of cynicism): worried about the family reputation. As soon as the old man and woman leave them "to their devices," her young officer whispers he needs to borrow money. To overcome a gambling shortage. She hesitates to tell him her financial situation. Outside it snows. He stays approximately 10 minutes. She follows him to the door. Wanting to put her hand out and touch his uniform. He turns and almost salutes without looking her in the face. A single snowflake falling on his pink-and-white skin. Before he walks down the curved driveway, between the snowbanks, to the road. She climbs the stairs to her flowered room. And sitting on the overly soft mattress under a heavy satin-covered comforter, she writes:

*Le mariage est une chose humiliante pour une femme.*

She half-sits with a start in the motel room in Kingston. Has she been dreaming? Outside the window the black water, the thin sliver of the moon's still shining angrily through the clouds. Also, the twirling spotlight, likely from the tower of the penitentiary. What's she doing in this town anyway? She straightens out her clothes, buttoning up the burgundy-red shirt over the pink cotton top.

Fortunately she can take a train. Trains are another form of communication (some would say, 19th century, like an old-fashioned narrative): a person can travel back and forth on the train between Montréal and Halifax nearly full time. Looking out the window at the shiny fields (green or white depending on the season); the shiny birch leaves turning up their little backsides in hope of rain; shiny dusks and dawns even in the greyness of the larger cities. Now, when she hits Montréal, she stays at the Y des femmes instead of venturing towards the east. Her friends, the revolutionaries, having grown hostile to her obsession; i.e., those who haven't dispersed to have babies. To become the socialist liberal parents of the marginal fringe of the coming generation. Anyway, at the Y, she hangs around the pool. Wearing sunglasses with white plastic rims.

She steps into the hall.

The chrome edges of the cigarette machine in the motel in Kingston are etched in that same terminal (end-of-day) light as dreams. Or as in when you wake from some heavy sleep not knowing where you are. Feeling only that you must never close your eyes. Because you'll be sucked back towards that damp and smothering place that appeared in your sleep. Keeping moving the best way to stay awake. Trains are full of narratives (although the days are over of conductors singing in the "lounges"). The stories of people's lives: that young woman (hatbox and fine hair in a bun) leaving Halifax (ca. 1860) allegedly in pursuit of a young officer. Modern version of same, arriving in the old Hollis Street station: wearing jeans and cowboy-style boots. In every period, women travelling all over, refusing to be rooted. Maybe that stuffy room at the old couple's could be stood, briefly, if daily going out for air. She could hire a calèche (they have them there for tourists).

Maybe she doesn't want to go to Halifax. She imagines a dusty road on the outskirts of a city. And that funny shiny house she once perceived, driving, with her parents, outside the city. The feeling of déjà vu the house gave (seen previously in a dream). A feeling somehow associated with the notion that life and death are unbelievably close. The shiny roof, the dead red brick so still against the grass, both alluring and repulsive. Thank god (if she resurfaces publicly in that former British garrison town, now modernized with high-rise buildings and under a sort of Constitution) her nosy mother's dead. Her father, too, who fell ill shortly after she left the university in Kingston.

"M'affranchir de mon père, de sa parole, n'est pas contraire à ma conscience," she wanted to tell various people offering their condolences at his funeral.

In the cheap-motel hall in Kingston, she notices she forgot her quarters. Retreating to her room, she sees (passing, in the mirror) how the black jeans define the firmness of her thighs leading to the crotch: women who don't eat often feel best about their bodies. Again she walks down the hall. Lining up her quarters on the chrome edge of the cigarette machine. One by one they slide into the slot. The place calls to mind a pool hall: baize-green rug; sparsely furnished except for a few flat surfaces disappearing in the darkness of the corners. A moosehead on the wall. She sniffs a new cigarette. Her favourite author, Colette, has taught her that the materiality of things sometimes is all that separates the human body from a terrible sense of nothingness. Which is why, when walking, Adèle often imagines each step as being towards the abyss of the future, her back bathed in light. Privately (she doesn't know why) she thinks of this perpetual motion as "memory's motor."

She takes out some matches. In this motel hall in Kingston, she could be any woman (25-30) buying cigarettes. You see them in the cities, long (or short) hair, walking on the streets. Deciding what to do. Looking for allusions, that is, attractive surface-images providing information on how to make an art out of their lives (not repeat their mother's). Bending her shoulders, also her back, and her knees in black jeans and boots, she takes a high step forward. Then another. Moving thus down the hall, her eye is drawn momentarily by the round numbers on the dial of the wall telephone. Maybe she should try for one more (failed?) communication. There must be a lot of fog between the motel and the military college.

Her hand rides absently up her stomach. Speaking of the materiality of the body, if she goes to Halifax, it will have to be even flatter. Because——she might as well dream on until it's time to catch the train; also, dreaming narratives covers up the pain—if her young officer won't go to her when she rents a room in Halifax, she will have to go to him. Yes, she'll have to be thin enough to don an officer's suit herself: blue tunic for some semi-dress occasion. Some occasion not requiring tickets. A gathering of the boys for an evening "mess" after an intramural game. The night not too warm and slightly misty. Cadets strolling up and down the spacious verandah. She could join them, strolling up and down, too. Though not stepping through the French doors into the huge reception room for drinks. Because, being an officer and a "gentleman," she'd have to remove her pillbox. Revealing the pinned-up bun of woman's hair hidden under it.

She loves the magic of illusion.

So to the verandah: she strides, dashing, euphoric, sure in this disguise she can accomplish anything. Marching up and down with a quick, nervous step. Her pink "officer's" cheek, her well-shaped lips glow in anticipation. Her hips more perfect, more suited to the tunic than ever his could be. He'll surely admire her courage. Expectantly, she eyes every cadet she meets. Her booted feet clacking sharply against the verandah's wooden floor. After a while, she leans against the wall, knee bent, boot sole against clapboard, an apparently leisurely pose the better to watch them passing. Such a "leisurely" pose is hard to maintain for long. She steps forward towards a group of young cadets talking. Getting up the courage to ask the youngest, nicest of them, to go inside with a message for Jack or John Christian. Except—he's there— putting out his hand to shake. She scrutinizes his face, unsure she recognizes certain traits. But he's stepping back angrily. Then leading her quickly to a misty corner of the neighbouring cemetery. She tries to establish eye contact. Predictably, he's saying she's outrageous. She moves to put her hand lightly on his chest. Or almost, because to actually touch would be totally unacceptable for two young officers. The letter in her pocket cries out for communication:

*Dear John: How hard it is to write.*

He: "You have shown a serious lack of respect towards my profession, my uniform and myself."

The letter: *I can't bear how you never try to reach me. How you do nothing to confirm our love's existence. Or that it's finished.*

He: "I am beginning to realize your relationship to reality is seriously messed up."

In the motel hall, she decides not to phone. A woman never gains by pressuring a man. Plus, it's getting close to train-time. The pain can always be absorbed. Continuing down the hall, it occurs to her that an obsession, if it is red, is more like waving flags at bulls: it makes them react violently. Example: him waving her at his family. She laughs, remembering her single visit to the house on the Arm. Later the very same day that he'd tiptoed to her chintzy blue room with his condom stuck on his stiff red prick, that aunt of his had looked at her as if she were a prostitute. She lies down on the motel bed, working up the memory. She seems to have been sitting on a dock in a bright red suit. Feeling so blissed out, she couldn't tell if she was awake or asleep. When some member of the family, probably aunty, announced the family jewels had been stolen. Adding that a boat had sunk and *you* (looking pointedly at Adèle) knew very well what was in it. Actually (Adèle thought)—she herself had been in it. But had floated up with the spring thaw. Now she was sitting on the dock, her red suit-jacket over her shoulders. A small and secret smile on her face.

She knew very well what "les bijoux de famille" meant in French.

He hates it when she follows him.

She turns over on the motel bed in Kingston, dozily. Time to get up and pack: the train going east leaves at midnight. The problem being that with the particular dizziness caused by hunger, hours can fly by just contemplating the possibility of action. At least she hardly ate, so now can buy the ticket to get to the address of her next welfare cheque. And possibly other revenue too.

She snuggles deeper, lying on her back. Imagining herself sitting up in hopes of shaking off the dizziness in her head. Gingerly, her feet will touch the floor. Opening up the suitcase, she'll start packing various sets of clothes: short skirt and tight military-style top covered in paillettes. Jodhpur pants and chiffon shirt. Both jockey shorts and lace undies. (Nor could anyone say the purpose of this combination of feminine and virile outfits.) For a hungry woman the suitcase is kind of heavy. She stands up straighter. Dragging it down the gravel road, under the single bulb lighting up the motel front, towards the station. Some young officers are cavorting on the platform. Boarding, she hardly notices.

Sitting in her seat, she can hardly keep awake. Getting even dozier with the train wheels clacking softly. A young officer with unusually large hips for a man goes down the aisle. She pays no attention. Leaning back on the seat dreaming of a woman travelling, dressed in red. At least a red shirt or some kind of red jacket over her shoulders. A woman seen often on the train between certain stations. A woman smiling in anticipation. For in a moment the conductor will announce:

"Mesdames, messieurs, nous arrivons à Montréal.

"Watch your step.

"Don't fall."

**(the sky is what I want)**

In the bar, someone puts on the *mambo* tape again.

It's true she's drunk too much.

She (Lydia) stares out. The sun has set one more degree. The sky, still a pale Aztec blue, distant, but full of meaning. Receding behind the fake metal pediment across the street. To the point, nearly, where it's totally washed out. Leaving a thick yellow haze at the level of the horizon. Her eyes (green) glance suspiciously beyond the rooftops. It's not natural for the dusk to be honey-coloured like that. She prefers to think of surfaces more tangible aesthetically: she means real people and what they can produce. The ochre pediment across the street carved unevenly: 1904. By a Jewish craftsman. Probably fleeing pogroms—

It's true, also, that in waiting, the space of melancholy can open up too much.

Lydia smooths her rich auburn locks, crisp blouse, dark skirt. A woman neither old nor young (she likes this neutrality of image). Likewise *relatively* sober. Sitting there waiting for that ring of happy night creeping towards the bar. Already darkening swags, rosettes, scrolls on upper façades. *Then* she'll be cool, collected. Closer to somnambulism, with its ease of movement over what's-to-be-forgotten. Than to (mild) drunkenness. Because, taking it, slowly. Easier.

She lights a cigarette. Raising her chin, so it won't look weak like the *mambo*-dancing woman's (still across the bar). Also, to avoid looking down at her fingers on the scarred tablecloth: slightly swollen, compared to how they were in the park this morning. The skin all unmarked and shiny, because detoxified. She'd been there since dawn. A little dizzy, having drunk only water and lemon juice for ages. Stepping so light she could float, past that striped house (its cornice bearing banal impressions of beaver, maple leaf). Lying in the grass, watching the pink light of dawn slap hard against the mountainside and flying gulls' bellies. Breathing in the greenness of the mist.

Then she saw the damned lumpy shadow, with the blanket thrown over it.

The *mambo* tune starts playing.

Lydia fills her glass. The woman from Halifax (again) crosses her line of vision. With that tirelessness she admires. The way every step she takes fills, with hope, the gap of the future. Stepping high across the tiles. The trace of her button breasts under the pink V-neck shirt followed critically by the regulars. The woman stands by the phone. Small smile on her mouth despite the frown between her brows. "Not positivist," thinks Lydia, "nor melancholy, either." Obviously aware there are two kinds of blues: sad, and I want sugar in my bowl.

"Possibly *too* ethereal," says a voice somewhere.

The *mambo* tape plays louder.

Lydia sips a little. Looking around unconsciously for a subject more tangible (more fixed in time). Peering behind the line of shadow, where Ralph the drunken sailor's standing up and sitting down, his war medals clacking loudly. Pointing to his glass. The regular who plays the video game all day, leaning on the counter waiting for some change. Likely simultaneously counting, with his mean little mouth, the number of carafons she's ordered. Double standards, also known as patriarchy. But she can easily ignore him. Being a woman who knows the importance of cultivating lightness (while attributing light its shadow). As a new approach to History. She thinks of her "brides" on the roof. Nanette (who deserves another chance). The woman from Halifax. In her cheap pink V-neck shirt, now getting up to pay. Curls a little messy. Pale ... *the way hysterics get in expending too much energy.*

Lydia straightens quickly.

That voice could be in her mind. Or else—in some dialogue going on beside her. But she's not going to be so sensitive to her environment (making her want drugs and alcohol as a means of self-defence). Earlier, in the park, it felt both suicidal and light as laughter. She thinks: "I'm beginning to resent the energy needed to combat it." IT being a trope for many things, social and political (trope's her favourite word). She smooths back her hair. Lighting a cigarette. Holding in her stomach: a woman (small, but attractive), waiting in a bar. For the greedy decade to give way to some new kind of History.

Her eyes narrow, reflecting, in the dim light coming from the window, that fish on the wall across the street, with EAST TIMOR written in it. Then in the corner of her gaze, the Portuguese woman in black skirt and white blouse (the one who looks like her) gets up to make a phone call. Herself a trope (Lydia thinks) for the displacement of people from continent to continent. Crossing the tiled floor. As if crossing that marvellous arched square in Lisbon by the twinkling bay. Or climbing the white-shadowed stairs of the Arab-looking quarter called Alfama towards the crest. Putting her quarter in and listening for a minute. Getting a busy signal. Or nothing. Likely feeling, as she hangs up (although she doesn't show it) the way a woman does in trying to forget she phoned someone who didn't want her. Or, any kind of memory tinged with regret.

On the tape deck the music starts again.

"Un carafon," calls Lydia (for lightness). Looking at the sky, increasingly ephemeral (streaks of pink and green and purple). Ignoring the regular at the video machine, who, at the sound of her voice, is smirking ostentatiously. The newer client, at least (white shirt, tweedy pants, despite the heat, who's been watching her more positively), must take her for what she is. A woman imagining a

History where anyone can enter (without getting murdered). Comprised of, say, small aesthetic details as much as wars and treaties. Like a *ruche* on a dress; or that little half-sun—sign of British empire, reduced down to size—on a cornice up the street; a Louis XVI grille on a flat-topped mansard leaning up beside it. Lower down, the wide azure beam flooding the front half of the bar. As the door opens and a French-speaking couple enters. Choosing a table, and settling in for an evening of pleasure. Moules, frites, un gros pichet de bière. The guy stretching his arm (like a cat's). Before lighting a cigarette from the huge package of Players on the checkered tablecloth. His companion leaning forward in expectation.

The *mambo* tape plays louder.

The woman from Halifax with her pale skin, dark eye-circles, crosses back to her table and leaves a tip for the waitress. Her skinny hips (in formerly tight jeans) then moving out the door. A little high, maybe, but knowing exactly where her ticket says she's going. Lydia thinks: "the essence of the traveller." Not traveller in the sense of that filmmaker who came in earlier from the Cooper building. Speaking loudly to his assistant (whose chair was rubbing the back of hers):

"I call this scene *He Shot His Bolt*. See [the guy had a slightly British accent] —a man and woman meet riding on a train. The woman's in a green wool dress with shoulder pads, you know, 40s-style; the man in uniform, although the war's over: it's 1949. They're getting really hot [his voice started sniggering]. Thinking the conductor doesn't see—he does—they sneak into the can. The woman says: 'Okay, penetration on condition that—.' The guy promises. But at the crucial moment the train hits a bump. And the poor guy, trying to pull out, does the opposite. Two more bumps, and, each time, he finds himself thrusting when he's moving to withdraw. Until he shot his bolt!"

Both the guys laughed.

The clock on the wall has a beer-ad for a face.

Outside two pregnant "girls" go by (a bumper crop this year). Their tender bellies in loose T-shirts and multi-coloured tights. Accompanied by a smiling hippie-looking guy. The clock says 7:55. "Un carafon," she calls again, impatient. Her eyes glancing, once more, above the rooftops. The clouds (when it's hot like this) so yellow they look like smoke. Reaching in and giving a tint of sulphur to the smoky bar. If only this were some less polluted century. Then the bar, with the same ray of light cutting down the middle, could be a hotel lobby, say in Halifax. In 1865. A woman, clearly some kind of traveller (Lydia's kind), entering the dark oak-panelled beery-smelling room. The woman, tall and slim, doesn't close her umbrella until she's sitting down. This was apparently a habit of the original Adèle H., the exiled poet's daughter, who arrived in Halifax about that time. Allegedly in search of a man who had promised her his hand (this turned out to be a lie: when their paths crossed on some Caribbean island she didn't even recognize him).

Lydia pours a little wine. Imagining a History from the point of view of women travellers. Women constantly in movement, the better to synthesize what they've left behind. Example: in the corner of her gaze, the *mambo-dancing* woman—who's obviously been to Cuba. Now standing at her table. In the cheap cotton shirt with fishes printed on it, waiting for the music. A sort of attitude *passionnelle*, one chubby arm extended, younger than the face.

Lydia sips slowly. Smiling at the thought that women travellers, like sleepwalkers, move unerringly. Always packing up, and going here and there. Also—by being into change—exerting great control on their existence. Because always able to choose the exact moment in which to re-become anonymous. Moving from International Hotel to International Hotel (she loves the redundancy of those words, "hotel" by definition suggesting "international"). Women also appreciate hotels for their absence of domesticity. Write entire chronicles from them. Or just sit watching sunsets from plate-glass hotel windows. Maybe in Varadero, Cuba. The scarlet hour just before the vacant utterly pale purple, when people go for drinks. The hotel, with its Bauhaus-style interior, was at its high point on the eve of the Cuban Revolution.

The music starts up.

That woman in the shirt with fishes printed on it, hair cut shorter on the sides, longer at the back, starts to do the *mambo*. A strain at the corner of her eyes despite the healthy tan. A little stiff in the shoulders. But starting to get into it. Lydia imagines her in the act of watching the brilliant sun slip towards the waves in Varadero. A small orchestra of Cubans setting up on the terrace. In search of tourist dollars. She sits there in her low-priced cotton dress on a leather sofa behind the plate-glass window. (Down a nearby

country road the arms of a very thin Cuban lead his ox
home.) No—she's just arriving from the airport, with a
black jacket over the shirt with fishes on it, black jeans
and boots. Lydia's eyes close, sensing some darkness under
the bright vacation surface.

But it's too late to stop.

Does she have her sister with her?

## DIS-MAY


*Mambo!*


What's absurd is life gets back to normal. After
you've lived through what you never (always) knew you
would. A cold, dark night. You're a little late. Hurrying,
because even at a distance, you can see the lights are off.
When they should be on. When the house should be
ablaze with the presence of your sister.

Walking across this hotel courtyard in Cuba, it's so
hot you feel a little silly in your black high-heeled boots.
Through an archway, the sea is boldly twinkling turquoise.
You step into the lobby made from four stone arches
posed with dépassé colonial smugness on the white beach.
Washing through them, a warm tangy sea odour full of
healing promise.
*Mambo!* someone calls.

There had been an omen. But, at first you failed to

grasp it. In fact, you didn't even see him coming down the street in the gently falling snow: a prettyboy in bleached hair dark at the roots, black leather suit and boots. You and the lesbian from Vancouver didn't see him as you walked and talked, the falling flakes whitening the dried flowerstalks along the sidewalk. Her voice saying, "Once you've done it that way, you can't go back." Meaning loving women. When this stranger you hadn't even noticed, coming from the opposite direction, leaned forward and pushed his face right up in yours. As if what other people thought could never stop him. Precisely as she said "you can't go back" and the two of you were laughing, his white face leaned over, boldly into yours. You could feel his breath. Before he straightened up and walked away grinning.

"There goes evil," one of you said.

*Mambo!* they call again.

Walking across this hotel terrace in the heat is like being in a postcard. With those Cuban men drinking at a table under a drooping, lazy palm. As in caricatures from some North American newspaper regarding productivity in "underdeveloped" countries. Laughing as you (in sweating black) and your sister drag your suitcases over the baking-hot terrace. Well, you're not the typical North American woman you look. You're closer to them philosophically than they probably think. If any still are communist (so many going hungry since the Soviets have fallen). True, before what happened happened, your interest in politics had already started to diminish, due to the lassitude of the 80s. Now, "post-trauma," feeling *quite* reactionary. Wear a curved knife in your boot. Are calling for the death penalty.

*Mambo, one, two.*

You drag your suitcase into the pavilion indicated by the tourist liaison officer's finger. Not Cuban, to your surprise, but Québécoise. A refugee from capitalism? (Cuba's nearly the only place left and sinking fast.) With gleaming teeth and golden tan, naturally. But in personality, quiet, kind of philosophical. Instead of bubbling over noisily like these tourist officers usually do. Maybe in this socialist country, tourism is less ... ridiculous. You enter the pavilion. Even with the shutters drawn, the brilliant light shining through the slats falls on a "modern" common space with cheap early-60s reddish-orange sofas and peeling paint. You kick open the bedroom door, given your hands are full and—

Tiny, airless, noisy. Not even a real room, really, but a small opening off a suite occupied by two boozy couples. A wife (in baseball hat) steps into the common space, sits on a sofa, and starts loudly mixing rum fizzes. Why do single women always have to fight to get treated with a minimum of decency? You and your sister race back, over the terrace. This vacation has to do its healing warming work of re-establishing some self-esteem. The Cubans watch, bemused. You enter the lobby (outside the open arch the turquoise sea is blinding) protesting loudly.

"Back in Montréal they promised us a good room.

"We need peace for medical reasons ..."

Peace, relatively, you had peace in your pretty house by the quiet snowy park. Where you came to live with your sister, not your real sister. But that's another story. Then in came chaos. Time in strips—

"May, may I ask you something." This was a joke between you because your sister is named May. "Did he, uh, have a white face with black circles under the eyes?" Leaning, as you walked down the snowy sidewalk, suddenly, pruriently into yours. But May's hands, and delicious arms, just starting to fill out, shook up and down impatiently. Didn't want to talk about it. God, they told you at the Crisis Centre: Never Repress Trauma. What else? Never Try To Defend Yourself Against An Armed Intruder. On the contrary: a person can always *do* something. If a woman doesn't, it's because she wants it. Oh why didn't you make her take those self-defence lessons they were offering at the Y?

Never mind. She'll talk sometime.

Now, in your high-heeled boots you march meaningfully over the Spanish-style courtyard. *One-two.* Up some stairs. Louise, the Québécoise tourist-guide, smiling white teeth in tanned—but not too much—moon face because she got permission from someone higher up to give you a large and airy room. (It helps you can speak to her in nearly perfect French, making you seem less anglo.) Windows looking over a garden of waving coconut trees. And of course, below, the sea. You and your little sister smile thinly at each other. Her blonde presence so suppressed, you think. It's like a shadow. You drink a thermos of Cuban water and collapse on the bed. Outside someone shouts:

*Everybody mambo.*

You get up.

The courtyard, again. Marble floors, those incredible Spanish arches, a gate with a little tinkling bell over it, and in the west the scarlet sunset. You and your sister among the dancers and the tables. Beached, showered, dressed, in pastel flowering skirts, white blouses, sandals. Yes, skirts. You're one dyke who prides herself on being able to move in all sectors of the population. Without revealing anything of her hidden inclinations. You mustn't be too obvious about that waitress in the hotel restaurant. She could get arrested. God she's cute. The way she makes so much out of the limited fashion resources of a non-consumer society. Almost boyish in her waiter's jacket with rolled-up sleeves, white shirt and brushed-back hair. Actually, something between that and an intriguing Russian lady from a spy movie ca. 1930. Especially when she smiles with her red red lipsticked lips. Pity certain things are forbidden (hidden) under "socialism."

To some degree, they are everywhere.

"*Mambo,*" shouts the dance teacher, clapping hands and leaning forward.

You look over the balustrade. Beyond the bell in its little alcove above the arch-shaped gate opening on the outer terrace just below. So strange to be somewhere where what's real is the fuchsia setting sun, the yellow rum-laced punches, the pale-green evening sea. That postcard stuff again, as if one could fictionalize reality. You turn and face the woman in the turban. Leaning back, shaking her breasts, laughing at the tourists' stiffness.

"*Mambo*," she shouts again.

"Let's dance," says your sister. Moving experimentally to the beat. Maybe in a minute. You're concentrating as you move towards a table for a nice relaxing drink—on how things could have gone so wrong. Besides, the *mambo*'s kind of retro. You pause for a minute. Oh, there's Yvette, that elegant older woman, also from Québec, you met yesterday. You push brusquely through the dancers towards her and her companions—in pastel-tinted dresses, silk scarves, serene, laughing. Intrigued from the first time you saw them: the bright sea light striking the outlines of their nearly patrician profiles by the dark stone wall of the hotel foyer. Like statues against the sky. "Where're you from?" you'd asked, smiling. Couldn't believe their answer: "Brossard," a ticky-tacky suburb.

You and your sister push towards their table. They, taking in your pretty skirts and blouses. So bright, so touristy, no one could ever guess you've been through hell. Or other hidden things about you: personal sexual choices. Maybe you're being punished. Maybe what went wrong is: you're a chameleon. Projecting an image of cute little typical single woman, briefcase, slacks. Running out for various contracts. Reserving your identity as a dyke for certain bars, cafés. Dyke's an essence that pales if hidden. Whereas if left in light is bright, assertive.

Skirting the marble-tiled courtyard, you're glad the sea is quiet. Last night that delightful little bell blew the prettiest little storm-warning you ever heard. You lay awake and watched your sister sleep. A wing of her white-gold hair over one eye. Hoping she wasn't dreaming. Outside the little bell rang, not louder and louder (it's too small), but more and more desperately. You opened the shutters (rather a gust of wind tore them from your hands). In the garden, the palms were lashing at the ground. And the waves so high. Lying back, you felt afraid. Afraid they'd climb the steps and reach the court-yard. Climbing higher until they hit your door.

"*Mambo,*" shouts the dance teacher, a shoulder suddenly leaning forward.

Just as you brush by her large body. Aware she's moving effortlessly, gently to the beat. Her whole being infused with rhythm, like the sea. That's what "rhythm" really means—not jerking the head or arm while the body stays static, the way the tourists do. You won't dance because the Cubans laugh at them.

You reach the table of Yvette, Renaude, Gina. Sinking into their perfumed warmth. Enjoying as you sit the loose weave of Renaude's strapless linen, Yvette's pale green with matching scarf around her neck, Gina's exuber-ant flowered print. With rings on their fingers and bells on their toes, they could make music wherever they go. That's a joke. They're 50 if they're a day, yet every time you glimpse them: dressed perfectly, enjoying themselves immensely. Your sister, a streak of red lipstick drawn rue-fully across her face, whispers in your ear: "It must be fun to be Yvette's kids. She makes funny squealing sounds when she's in the water and the big waves come."

FUNNY, it's really smooth as glass now after last night's storm. An air of innocence, as if nothing happened. Calm, too, that night you and the lesbian from Vancouver started out for Molivo's. The late spring snow falling on the sidewalk, padding everything. And through the branches, the cross on the mountain shining, fluorescently absurd. Then that creep intruded. Just by the block of elegant greystones with wood- and plaster-work, fireplaces, oak mantels, brass and marble tiles. Looking on the park the way they do, it's the country in the city. Except, things still happen in the alleys. That kid you saw shooting out of the baker's parking lot. Slipping on the ice and getting up in a single movement. Followed by the sleek black car with sinister, tinted windows. Likely running for his life.

How does she fit what happened into her continuum of development? The way that creep bent the latch so she couldn't lock it. STOP THINKING! Except—watching her on the beach earlier you noticed her lips (so full, so sensual, men always leer at her in subways) were white, turned in. Because that Cuban entertainment director, Alberto, said: "Une belle fille. Ici, c'est automatiquement 10 ans de prison si on touche à une fille comme ça." She looks younger than she is. Especially now. Staring straight ahead, her face stony. Towards the sea so blue, you can't see the line where water becomes sky.

"*Mambo!*" cries the dance teacher, clapping. Whole body forward hips moving almost imperceptibly waiting for the needle to fall on the old-fashioned record. Some younger Cubans, leaning on an arch. The *mam-bo's* for the tourists.

The courtyard again. Yesterday or tomorrow. Time in strips. You step (no one's looking) to the *mam-bo* rhythm. Left foot, right arm, a pivot of the hips. Promising, as you move, not to mess up like earlier. With a foolish display of panic because you'd knocked and knocked at the hotel-room door (knowing she was there). But no answer, so you're calling her name, *May. May.* Almost screaming, nightmare visions of what happened back in Montréal, when you came in and found her unconscious ———. Until she opens, exclaiming furiously, "I was in the bathroom."

Maybe Yvette does sense something. The way she scrutinized you from under her tight, unpuffy eyelids (unpuffy means good kidneys, the seat of courage) on the beach, this morning. After one more storm. The tiny little waves were twinkling quite relentlessly. Like so many shiny little fish hypnotizing, hypnotizing till your eyes hurt. Then Yvette appeared in brown-and-white-striped strapless bathing suit. Pleated tastefully over a tummy that had sheltered five kids. Elegant yet motherly. "Bonjour," she said. "Mon Dieu, qu'elle est belle, votre soeur. Elle a de belles dents. Moi, je regarde toujours les dents."

You lay back and waited. You could hear the other women from Brossard spreading out their bright towels discreetly at a distance. Then, one of them was bobbing on the waves. Floating on her back, hair tucked in bathing cap. Her ample chest in red and white moving seaward on its rocking turquoise mattress. Their talent for squeezing happiness out of every minute, totally admirable. You've seen signs they also have their troubles, but they never waste a second, walking on the beach, talking to everyone they meet, always wine at dinner although it costs extra.

You head for their table.

"Voulez-vous un punch?" Yvette turns regally, courteously, in your direction. Back perfectly straight even when she sits. You've always noticed, in Québec, the better posture of the French. You straighten up yourself. Around the courtyard's edge, the tourists in their mint and yellow wear. Tanned now: an improvement on reality. The dance teacher claps and everyone jumps up as, in the fruit-scented air, the dance tempo suddenly changes to *cha-cha-cha*. A pair of striped short-shorts and long tanned legs in high-heeled sandals minces forward confidently. Beside hairy feet in sandals. Your sister tugs your arm. You say maybe you'll try when it's time again to

*Mam-bo*. Because you have to lighten up. *One-two pause OOONPH!* seems to be the beat. You smile at her teasingly, given her reticence on the beach when a man (enormous cock in skimpy bathing suit) produced a limbo stick. Yvette having volunteered immediately. Completely unself-conscious, shaking shoulders and bending back, crotch-first under the lowering stick. You stepped forward, too. The combo of musicians (actually from a prison) picking out a rhythm while you squeezed under at a fairly high level. But you're stiff as a board, your shoulders crunched forward so the chest concave, as if protecting something. May, concerned as usual that people might see the two of you are tarnished, sidled forward and whispered in your ear:

"Please stop."

Yvette's manicured hand around her own personal rum bottle spikes up the punch a little. What you have to stop is your wanting to be comforted. Wanting to lean your head on Yvette's soft chest, and feel the warmness of her belly against your face. You look at May's lovely caressable cheeks, which you could not protect. Sipping Yvette's punch. The tourists dancing more and more frenetically *one-two one-two one-two one-two Agh OOONPH.* The pretty sea lapping peacefully on the beach. Yvette beside you, shoulders down and back, in beige sheath, with double row of pearls. Next to her, the proud bleached head of Renaude, suddenly blurting out: "My son's leaving home to live with his amie. She wants him for his money." You notice her white dress has a large turquoise stripe to one side up the front: strong, authoritarian. A little tipsy, she gets up to dance. Gina, heavy, indulgent, leaning over in her décolleté talking, talking intensely to Alberto. The single one, always planning some excursion.

You get up and try to take a picture of your precious blonde sister. Watching the sunset's rosy fingers grasp the turquoise water. Just above her head the little bell tingles in the wind. But not too much. Not threateningly. Another day gone. In the picture, it turns out, she's cut off by the frame. You go to bed. Late into the night, in the little courtyard, the music plays. Occasionally, someone calling joyfully, victoriously (just as you—nodding off—sink your curved knife deeply into the heart of that creep, that prettyboy you followed up The Main. Having seen him from a taxi, standing on a corner, shaved head, perverse). Someone calling:

*Mam-bo*—until

It's tomorrow. Through the shutters the slanted yellow light shines in from the salt-washed garden. At last a perfect day. Too bad you paid for that excursion, when it's ideal for the beach. May opens her eyes and says: "Time goes too fast. I have to get a better tan before we go home." You smile reassuringly. Yes, my sister, we shall savour every healing minute. Refusing to divide our lives into after and before. Just keep walking over stupid fearful memories, with an air of self-assurance. What makes you furious is you were at such a high point last winter. As the short days started getting longer. Feeling centred. Moving up The Main in leather jacket (brown), jeans and boots. Your sister, too, gorgeous, cheeky, like young girls should be. Except—he stole the jacket after he slipped back the latch and put his foot in the door—

Damn, the minute you open your eyes, this chaos starts. To stop it, you just have to put your feet on the cold stone floor. And look in the mirror. God—the frame is tacky: 50s-style with lacquered slightly rounded strips of wood up each side. It looks funny hanging on the old stone wall like that. Your face stares out, darker than you thought. You know you're not as tough as you look. The darkness of the eyes ... Behind you, she's propped on pillows reading Agatha Christie. Why isn't she jumping up like she used to? You know the answer—

You turn, smiling gaily. Step through a little vestibule that opens on an enormous bathroom. Old-fashioned fancy brass fixtures, huge low shower-bath lined with pastel tiles. Someone like Zelda Fitzgerald could have thrown off her silk robe there, shaking her white shoulders, and stepping in. After, May will take her turn. You'll both put on your new white shorts, down to the knees, striped T-shirts, neutral, touristy. Arriving a little late in the breakfast room, carefully dressed in your limited summer wardrobe. Smooth, relaxed: it's amazing what a little sun can do.

The two of you step forward (no music in the morning).

The breakfast room is full. Side tables resplendent with citrus fruits. Limes, juicy grapefruits, oranges still slightly green in spots because ripened on the branch and not in some refrigerated warehouse. (It all goes for the tourists: they're desperate for the currency.) You step past Louise, the Québec-Cuba liaison woman, quarter-moon face in profile, brilliant teeth sinking into a brilliant green lime. For breakfast she always eats limes, yogurt, fresh juice. *No coffee!* That's probably why her features glow and glimmer under her light tan and sunstreaked hair. A big woman, those rolling hips more like many here than women in Québec. You mean, Québec *now*, since modern beauty standards have substituted the pubescent ingénue for the solid bodies valued two generations back. When women, as mothers of the threatened nation, had huge families. Your eyes seek out Yvette, Renaude, Gina. That skinny Cuban waitress leans against a pillar. Things more open now between the locals and the tourists. What a smile. But you're too tempted to go near her—

"Stop staring," whispers May, scanning the room

uneasily from under her straying wing of hair. "And push your chair in when you get up. Everybody does."

She didn't used to be so self-conscious. Actually, sort of the reckless type. Before that night, shaking violently in your arms. And your shocked thoughts: the inner woman screaming *It's not possible.* The two of you like an image in some porno film. Then the symbols started clashing, senselessly. Everywhere you went the air was white with anger. As in that screeching symphony of traffic jam, walking up The Main the very next day. A small thin voice in the intervals of brakes squeaking, in the streets, the horns honking, keening: "Mutilated body, mutilated body." High above the traffic.

Here, there's hardly any traffic.

Everything is calm …

The two of you run out, holding sticky bread, and climb into a wagon. An oldish Cuban tractor pulls it, mostly full of pensioners, along the empty dusty road. You lean back, wide shorts flapping, feeling ridiculously pro-tected. Like some 19th-century English-novel heroine trav-elling in India. You'd rather be talking to that attractive Cuban ménage à trois you see walking along the sidewalk: two young women, arms tightly laced around the hand-some, curly-haired guy between them. You stare at the darker of the two, short hair, scarf around her neck, imag-ining her preference. Stare back at the road. Between all the liver-spotted hands raised up to snap photos you glimpse Yvette, Renaude, Gina right up front. Almost ironically demure in fresh white dresses, summer scarves. From a vacant humble window, a rather lazy

*Maam-bo.* Slow

Like the tempo of this wagon, crawling past a cavernous café: dark white space, tables, 50s Chev fins parked outside the door. A great time gap. Your sister stands, her face shadowed by some leaves, peeking through her Polaroid. Trying to snap an old man on the verandah of a rambling blue house. Not renovated yet. They're slowly renovating all the buildings here (*were,* before perestroika caused a lack of goods). Starting, naturally, with the army installations. Housing those beautiful soldiers who run half-naked on the beach. May smiles at the old man gazing sardonically from his white stubble at the tourists' cameras. There have always been turista. She pulls the picture from her Polaroid. All she's got in the white frame is the striped pole that holds the little wagon's sheltering awning up.

The tractor crawls around a wall. Below—a perfect beach, green palms, the sea. They say the ideal time for tanning is the morning—now it's nearly noon. You could jump off and call a taxi. Except you don't want to hurt the entertainment director's feelings. God, since when did you get so nice? Certain women, when frightened, like small animals become slavishly obedient. Back home your eyes had got in the habit of turning *left and right, left and right,* walking on The Main. Like one of those little mechanical dogs with turning head and lit-up eyes they put in car rear-windows. Looking for that creep. Almost wishing he would come back, now you have that pocket in your boot for a knife.

No, fuck, you don't wish that.

The tractor labours forward. You see a long groomed walk, winding among flowers to a glass-walled lobby. Through the glass: low leather chairs, white supporting columns, another glass wall, the perfect brilliantly white beach strewn with strange horse statues, leading to the sea. Right out of Ayn Rand—you mean, American-style decadence from before the revolution. You stare, momentarily dazed. Much as you hate the concept (the rich coming to exploit the underdeveloped nations), sitting in that lobby looking at the horses would make you feel like one of those androgynous-looking heroines from a 40s film. Which you could kind of use right now.

"I want a swim," says your sister, standing up again. Staring down the flower-bordered walk through the glass lobby at the twinkling turquoise sea. But Alberto's leaning over, chatting, chatting (in perfect French he learned on the radio—what radio you wonder?). Giving you the History of this International Hotel. Exclusively for East Germans until 1988. So they kept the best places for the communists. Well you can't blame them. You take a deep breath. Your sister staring stonily ahead. You can see this dragging on the whole afternoon. When all she wanted was a good tan, the better to go home feeling beautiful. The little wagon climbing climbing. To a point of suspension far above the beach (the pensioners clamouring for a drink). Rising up in the packed jerky elevator of a cheap-looking high-rise hotel to the penthouse bar. You and May trying to go down again, but it doesn't seem to work; you even try the stairs but the exit doors are locked. Meaning you'll sit there, listening to the pensioners complain

(Yvette, Renaude, Gina have completely disappeared).
Thin voices rising through the air-conditioned air, because
the punch is weak. While from her shadowed eyes May
looks accusingly at you. And you look back, helpless. Sit
there, staring through all that sunny air towards the distant line of beach. Then

It's dusk again. Another day gone. And again with
your darling sister (who's repressing all her feelings) leaning over the railing of your hotel balcony. Looking beyond
the gateway with the little bell above at the palms blowing
with the rhythm of the waves. The soft down of her perfect rounded cheek glistens rosily against the sunset.
"Bonita," says a passing chambermaid in black cotton
skirt and white blouse, the uniform of service people here.
The palm trees are waving quicker, like grass skirts. Sure.
Bonita. But they don't see what you see. The black circles,
heavy shaded eyes—immediately, in the passport photo,
taken a day after, you could see her cool and daring brow
had (temporarily) changed.

You turn your similar profile seawards. Over the
blush waves some heavy clouds are gathering. You feel a
black one's hanging over you, too. First the—incident. So
you go away and her goal is a great tan (to regain some
self-esteem). Then you waste the day and now a storm is
blowing. You never seem to do the right thing by her. At
Molivo's Restaurant (that night it happened) you kept getting up and going to the phone which hung on the wall
near an exotic-fish tank under a pretty plant. Ringing
always busy. Not to worry. Besides, you were trying to get

some strokes from that lesbian from Vancouver about some poem you'd written. Who kept trying to skirt the issue, as subtly as only the daughter of a British colonial officer brought up in the drawing rooms of Asia could. You ordered wine and made one more allusion.

*Mambo!* someone shouts on the terrace below.

To get over trauma you just need to keep moving. *One-two, one-two.* Descending the balcony stairs. Walking over the Cuban sunset reflected on the courtyard floor. Sniffing the rising tide which fills the air with its healing mist of salt. Towards the shadow of the arcade, where, oh there they are, the women from Brossard. They must have got off that stupid wagon somewhere along the way. You should have stuck with them—

The dance teacher claps, picking up the rhythm.

You step, determined, across the rose-tinted tiles. A breeze still sweet but strong blowing on your cheek. In the courtyard a gust of wind makes the little bell ring. You walk more quickly, followed by your blonde sister, towards the table of Yvette, Renaude, Gina. Unusually straightfaced, dignified, almost formally dressed. They must be going somewhere. Yvette in linen, pearls. Gina in sheer mauve with matching bandeau around her head. Renaude, her bleached hair frizzed by salt, watery blue eyes and lipstick drawn recklessly across her face, is getting up to dance. Drink in hand, still thinking about her son. At lunch, she eats nothing but cheese et un peu de raisin. The big meal always in the evening, with her two men. Now ... She shrugs. Her smile over-bright on the coarse, tanned skin. A face so masculine that, if you'd seen it on Ste-Catherine or The Main, you'd have thought she was in drag.

"*Mambo*," shouts the dance teacher. Leaning back, wiggling her shoulders, shaking her breasts, smiling provocatively at those trying to do the same. But the tourist women's breasts won't move separately, loosely from the shoulders the way the teacher's do. Bodies incapable of picking up the discombobulated rhythm, African, played with the left hand, under the more stylized melody of the Spanish, played with the right. You watch, cosy, by the curve of Yvette's arm. Marvelling at the beauty of the Cubans. That woman and her tiny identical daughter doing the perfect rhumba by an old apartment building. Winding, winding to the floor. Or those young soldiers whose rippling every-shade-of-brown-to-white bodies swim miles through the sea daily. Then get out and run in skimpy bathing suits, back along the beach. Yvette looked to see if you were interested. You were—enough to leer a little.

But Yvette, Renaude, Gina are getting up. Heading towards the gate under the little bell. Going to eat shrimp in an expensive restaurant tower. Then on to some show at, where else, the International Hotel: "The History of the Cuban Revolution," said Yvette, pretending to look dubious. *From Humiliation to Self-Appreciation.* But they always know what's good. Maybe you'll see that showgirl who was leaving a side door of the International Hotel as the tractor pulled away earlier. Perfect coffee skin, shiny blue-black hair braided over each ear.

In the courtyard the little bell clangs harder. Really, there's no use staying in the hotel room with its cheap orange bedspreads, stone walls, dwindling supply of Agatha Christie novels. Mooning over how the weather's going to be tomorrow. When you could join Yvette, Renaude, Gina at the International Hotel. You glance over at your sister to see if she looks interested. Strange how you're drawn to that place. If you could go and sit in a white dress in its glass lobby, like Greta Garbo in an old movie, you're sure you would feel comforted.

Tense and strained, you stand on the dimly lit terrace waiting for your sister to nod approval. A cold quarter-moon rising from the sea. "Provided," you say (prissily), "that a socialist country can put on a cabaret that's non-offensive sexually." May says, faintly, she'd rather dance herself. But looking round the now-deserted courtyard, you point out reasonably that there's no music playing. And the two of you step out beneath the violently tinkling bell. She wearing a gash of dark lipstick, to look older so they'll let her in. Along the sidewalk's edge the red flowers blow as if dancing to some wild Cuban music. You note she looks tired. But you, too, have needs to fulfil. Briefly, you consider a taxi, but what if the taxi suddenly veered off to a deserted beach with no recourse.

Twice would be the death of you.

You climb on the bus. Above the driver, a picture of Lenin. Outside you see nothing. The bus hurtles down the utterly dark road, while you imagine some sleazy detour that will cause you no end of trouble. At the same time hating how conventional you've become. Considering, two weeks back, you were still the cocky leather-jacketed dyke strolling up The Main. Before that junkie pimp ————. At least—he had a hooker for a girl-friend. Because, one day, a week after what happened happened, you see this young girl, perfect full breasts, blue shag wig, on the corner soliciting in *your* leather jacket. You just had to follow her to find him. You checked the knife in your boot. Then felt a kind of lassitude ...

Oh, the bus is stopping. The beautiful cabaret dancer (who happens to be sitting near the front, keeping you from panicking completely) stands up. Plus the two of you. The driver waves you back, it's only a service entrance. You crane your neck to see the glass walls and inner marble columns. "Look," you whisper to your sister, who seems kind of listless. The two of you get up. The wind in the black night stiffly whipping up your summer skirts as you step towards the entrance of the stunning Bauhaus-style foyer. Exactly as expected. A woman, more like Dietrich than Garbo, in blue silk, leaning on a column—

But your precious sister has drifted towards the cabaret: Arabian-night ceilings, deep red plush, blue horses prancing across the arch of the stage. Tables filled with Russians, Italians, Germans. A maître d' nearly stopping you. Before nodding politely, bowing ingratiatingly low. Maybe he's being cynical: it's a criminal offence to bring an under-age woman to a club like this. You'll end up in jail for corrupting adolescents. *That* would be ironic.

You just keep moving. Filing in behind Yvette, Renaude, Gina, all eyes on them, as they move dignified towards a table. You feel so proud as Yvette's warm, reassuring presence settles next to you. Good beige linen draped gracefully over a body that has strengthened with the giving. Up at dawn to walk. Stopping to watch the little Pioneer Children with their red scarves do their morning exercises. "Here they really know how to teach them self-esteem," she said at breakfast. Nibbling at her one toast and sipping her one coffee. Not much energy intake for a mother of five who works as well. No traumatic stains on them, either.

"Oh look," you whisper to your sister (wishing she would smile), "the show's starting." The emcee bows deeply under the arch of painted horses. "Ladeez and gentulmen," (in American showbiz English, then several other languages), "we're proud to present *The History of Cuba from Early Times Until the Revolution*. First [a rush of cabaret music], The Slave Period!" The beat is fabulous. African congas and women in long grass skirts moving in a rolling motion. Yvette, in the spirit, waving her lush, maternal arm, ordering a complicated drink: coconut milk, crushed bananas, rum, something bright green.

"Maybe," you whisper to her, "soon they'll do the *mam-bo*." For the beat is changing to a combination of African and flamenco. History (under the blue horses) ushering in the Spanish period. Men in fancy white suits dancing in a sexy side-step way. Across the table, Gina's purple-clad body bouncing up and down chaotically. Next to her Renaude, smiling sadly. Her bright lipstick still plentiful on her strangely masculine face. Suddenly blurting out: "Sa petite amie n'était pas si intéréssée, avant qu'il trouve une job. Mais, tu sais, les filles et l'argent ..."

You can't believe her jealousy. But History's in the American period. When the *mam-bo*, starting in Havana, rose to a frenzy of popularity in places like New York. Everyone trying to do that movement—the naughty pivoting of the hips, while the legs and arms do something else completely. Cubans leaving by the hundreds to make money in clubs, *el norte*. Under the blue horses, the dancers raise their ruffled skirts, twisting their pelvises towards the audience in some other kind of dance. You can feel your little sister staring unhappily at the empty bottom of her glass. The dancers drop their skirts. Clothed in G-strings, they're scampering up a scaffold, their feather headdresses tickling the blue horses' tummies. Yvette looks at May's troubled face. Yes, you'd leave but—

But—Yvette gets to her feet. Then you notice everybody is. Drifting out. Because on stage they're singing about the Cuban revolution (it's 1959). Heads together, swinging to a slightly Latin beat. You're aware of your little sister's sadness as you drift out with them: if only you'd have known such a thing would happen, you'd never have stayed so late at Molivo's. Holding forth about the qualities of your writing. Later, you looked at the horoscope to see if there'd been warning. *February 18: A bouncy Leo will bound into your house and make a real mess.* Nothing clear there. You pass the Ayn Rand leather sofa and open the glass door.

God it's dark. Along the walkway leading towards the unlit road those red-skirted flowers that grow everywhere are dancing, even more wildly than before. In the sinisterly high wind. You watch them while waiting for some mode of transportation to show up. Wondering what keeps them from dropping in exhaustion? Or their petals from flying off chaotically? Clearly this time a very serious storm. A person can't be safe anywhere. If it's not nature, it's whatever happens in the city.

But life gets back to normal.

The proof is you're soon in your hotel without a single incident. Stretched comfortably on the orange bedspread (in the courtyard a plant has blown over, and the little record-player that plays the *mambo* record sits unplugged). Thinking of how they make everything so easy. Yvette, hand on chin; Renaude, leaning on one spike heel, still preoccupied, no doubt, with son; Gina, slightly drunk: in front of the glass foyer. Their light clothes in profile against the blackness of the sky. The three of them like a family, in roles of mother, father, child. Renaude suddenly stepping forward with her pink and watery smile. And flagging down an empty chartered bus. Its old leather seats dating from the 50s.

You stretch out more comfortably. Smiling, feeling your sister's stronger than you thought. Even if—in the bus coming back—she looked sad and tired. Making you want (again) to put your head on Yvette's shoulder. To ask: what if May has permanent effects? You sat up straighter, shaking off the memory. That cop, after, looking at you sarcastically: "Peut-être la prochaine fois sera-t-elle mieux surveillée." You straightened even more. The bus descending a very steep corniche. So dark, you couldn't tell where you were except to know it's down. Yes, she's okay. Didn't *she* get up and say the very next day:

"I wasn't too impressed with his knife."

Now, watching her sleep with the fragile bell tinkling as loud as it can beyond the door, you start to feel
calmer. As if your rage is leaking out to greet the white
foam frothing. There, behind the closed shutters, promising to never again let rage give way to fear. Or, dismay
(you add), because the last thing your little sister said
before going to sleep was: "Tomorrow I want to sit in the
sun, then take dance classes."

But morning. And even with closed shutters you can
hear the angry waves pounding on the beach beyond the
wall. Your feet step on the cold stone floor and you pull
sweaters from the suitcase. You look out the window at the
palm trees blowing like frenzied skirts. At the wave-lashed
beach and storm-washed sky. "A little early-morning walk
will do us good. 'The early bird always gets the worm,'
your grandpa used to say. You can get a tan right through
the clouds." You pull back the covers laughing, tickling,
the way sisters do in times of peace.

She's not a complainer. Rather the determined type
who quietly bears her pain. This could be a problem: they
say a person has to talk a trauma out in order to recover.
Now, walking on the beach with her head down, you can
feel her disappointment. She loves the sun so much. She
has this picture she carries around with her of a chubby
baby, all sun-dappled. Held by a woman in a sun-dappled
dress. Their smiles also spotted with the dapples of leaf
shadows as they walk under a huge tree on a gloriously
sunny day. And she, the perfect chubby baby, is smiling,
smiling, laughing, laughing, holding her fist forward.

Yes, you could learn a thing from her. Keep interested in the little things, despite whatever obstacles and disappointments. You grab her hand, and move *one-two* as if to a *mambo* beat. You and your precious sister marching on the beach for your morning constitutional. Marching towards the point on which stands (you think) the International Hotel. The waves so high, sometimes you have to walk around them, sometimes right through the angry froth boiling up your ankles. She bends over to catch a piece of driftwood. Her naked pink heels under nice calves, firm buttocks, sinking in the sand. A piece of seaweed making her leg look both strong and vulnerable.

"It'll take a chunk from your lives," the lesbian from Vancouver said.

No it won't. You just have to keep moving. Thank god it's nearly breakfast. Maybe you'll see the red-lipped waitress. On the beach you and your precious one interrupt your march and turn back. Sliced orange, sliced grapefruit, gooey French toast, scrambled eggs, syrup, yogurt, limes, coffee (a group of hungry Cubans waiting on the verandah). You grab her hand and start running through the froth.

You're going to kill that lugubrious creep, with the knife in your boot. So you can continue to be that carefree women-loving woman you were before. Your feet pounding on the wet, cold sand, you think about how, suddenly, in front of the crummy bar with the plastic checkered tablecloths, he'll be standing. Holding a cigarette package between his thumb and forefinger. You'll pull your knife and—*whoosh*. Except if you do that, everyone will know.

Also, you'll go to jail and she'll be in a worse mess than even now. You look at her, who's slowing down. Who's saying vaguely, accusingly, she hopes at least tonight she'll get a last chance to learn the

*Mam-bo*

You lean forward, to reassure her you'll dance with her. Things are definitely getting better. You point out a place in the sky where a purple ray of light shines through the rushing frowning clouds. Some people turn out even stronger after trauma.

"Mais si tu dis ça," said another feminist back home, "Cela veut dire que cette aggression a été une bonne chose."

*AIEEEEEEEEEEEEEEEEEEEEE.* You start running. The waves crashing higher, so you have to press against the stone wall, to not get washed back as the swell recedes. Your little sister right behind. You climb the wet steps and head down a dark hall towards the dimmed light of the breakfast room. Dark, like that horrid penthouse bar. Like Molivo's, when while phoning you looked at the dusky window scene: not dark, exactly, but colourless to the point of sinister. Old stone fortifications. Beyond which a bridge-like construction site with a crane standing unused on it. Standing, waiting, waiting for that lesbian from Vancouver to acknowledge you as a poet. While, at your house, that junkie creep—

You pause for a minute. The pores of your back still longing for the violent salty air behind you. While, through the breakfast-room door, you see the profile of the tall skinny waitress. Leaning back against a table laden with piles of fresh peeled grapefruit. Also Louise, the Québec-Cuba tourist liaison officer, that is, the profile of her quarter-moon cheek sucking on a lime. And (in the background) Yvette, Renaude, Gina graciously pulling out their chairs and sitting down. The waitress smiles slightly with her red lips. Her black hair falling over one eye. You want to be lying with her on the beach. You step forward. Look behind.

My god where is she? Your sister—

**(the sky is what I want)**

What if she screamed out loud?

Lydia looks, embarrassed, around the bar. Outside the sky, still paler, with its slightly honeyed tint. And the bar's grown so hot with accumulated heat that glasses and bottles are streaming with condensation. The bar door opens violently. Injecting some loud-mouthed American tourists in bright Bermuda shorts. She lifts her damp glass and holds it to her cheek. Her eyes, for relief, seeking the darker, cooler reaches of the room beyond the line of shadow (inching towards the window as the sun retreats). Behind that line, Ralph, for once, sips quietly. Almost envious of his place in the dark, she rubs the cool (empty) glass against her skin (careful not to smudge the makeup).

But—what if someone heard?

She thinks: "it would be like reading a really embarrassing passage from my diary out loud." That one about *Shiny Genitals*. Of course, it depends on how you handle it. She glances up at the crookedly drawn 1904 pressed out of the metal ochre-coloured roof-trim across the street. Remembering the times she let it unaesthetically hang out all over. Being too direct (example: in the portrait of Nanette). Or, writing in her diary she had to free herself of someone, of some memory, of some stupid repetitive behaviour *the better to be me*. Under that last entry crossed out in blue ink, she'd written: *Dreamt last night I had Lesbian Sex (i.e. a passionate embrace)*.

Lydia laughs abruptly. What does it matter what anybody knows? It's no crime to make up portraits of patrons in a bar (eavesdrop a little). She looks around discreetly: the Portuguese woman in white blouse and dark skirt, like hers, is getting up to try her phone call again. Again crossing the tiled floor. Blue and white like the tiles on that square in Lisbon, where the air (brighter than anywhere) lightens people's faces. Head high, cigarette close to mouth, exhaling rapidly. Putting her quarter in and listening for a minute. Hanging up because, still, a busy signal. Or nothing. Smiling in retreat. Sitting down and smoking.

Lydia does the same. Inhaling deep into the gap of the centre. Thinking: "to cover emptiness, embarrassment, you just have to face each moment as if exploded from the previous." Like her "brides" on the roof—about to have a party. With haircuts that push easily into place. Their scent, intoxicating but leaving little trace. Which is how they want it. Only hitting memory nodes when, for reasons of aesthetics (life and art are one) a little melancholy's required. She imagines them behind those sprouting orbs or swordpoints, rising from cornices and pediments in mock aggression towards the sky. Nanette, perfect, considering circumstances; Adèle, of Halifax (achingly familiar). It's true—the *mam-bo*-dancing woman stupidly spoiled pleasure on the trip to Cuba, by continually recalling she'd become (by proxy) an unfortunate statistic. Not that Lydia blames her. But she never focuses on statistics.

She prefers another approach to History.

"*Borrego*," says a voice in Portuguese, ordering his dinner.

"Hussein's fascist," from the American tourists' table.

She focuses on the music. Also keeping down (with a gesture of her hand) an inner voice saying: "things happen randomly to women no matter what they do." Tapping lightly with her fingers to the slightly Latin beat (Ralph does the same—but banging): a woman (attractive), waiting in a window for some other kind of History. Comprising dream (multiple intuitions, possibilities) plus reality. Like the 13 Aztec heavens—all stacked up and graded in many different colours from dark earth to sky. Or, like those silhouettes going by the glass, glowing mysteriously at the edges: tough women cutting across the pellicule of dusk. As decided as in the Cocteau movie where the heroine goes to meet the devil.

Lydia (herself) pushes back her chair. Full breasts in white shirt (in the movie, the woman's shirt was striped, with short raglan sleeves). Stepping towards the cigarette machine. Aware a client (not the one in tweeds, who's given up and gone) is taking in the beauty of her contours. The gracefulness of her gait. The swing of her shoulders. There's a pause in the tape—

"*Maestro, je t'aime,*" says a voice. Then a sort of tango.

She sits down smoothly. Kind of planing out (in her system, the right amount of alcohol). Entering a spell. Until all she sees is the exterior of things. Exterior equals real. As if the eyelids had atrophied, letting in an overdose of impressions. So that in the bar the sound of tinkling of glass, cool, refreshing in the escalating heat, is a counterpoint to the music. The din of clients, ordering themselves another, as loud and happy as spectators cheering at the Forum. The movement of their heads, enforced by the intensity of the last rays of light, taking on the rhythm of performance.

Soon she'll order coffee to draw it out a little. Also, to maintain that unobtrusiveness of stance required of a woman observing various layers of society (from her place in a bar). She glances towards the regulars—one of whom (the failed writer at the video machine) glances back at her. With the same mock-disgusted look he had for the woman from the hospital detox centre earlier: bleached blonde hair, pale skin, orangey-red lipstick. Fur coat draped on her arm, despite the heat wave. Drinking Perrier after Perrier and smoking up a storm. Standing up and declaring suddenly, loudly: "Tell Jimmy I still love him."

(Jimmy, the barman, giving her the finger.)

Then: "Oops, sorry." Before going out the door.

Which door now opens, revealing a paranoid guy looking left and right. Talking to himself:

"I've got thousands of enemies."

Then two dykey-looking women against the wash of ever-paling sky.

Lydia loves the way they're standing: close, but not touching. All charged up erotically. Believing as she does in the beauty of deferral (unfortunately, one of them's too obvious in her way of dressing). The longer you wait, the better it feels when you finally do it. Some people even give it up for ages. Lydia wonders (guiltily) if the *mam-bo*-dancing woman, now going out the door, appearing fairly neutral in fish-printed shirt and loose black culottes, is into sex again. They say rape or any trauma can for a time really murder feeling. Of course, it was her sister—

"Un carafon," calls Lydia, her voice rising easily above the cacophony of the bar.

Breathing rapidly, deeply, to stay in her state of somnambulism-almost: head in the clouds, feet on the ground. Which state permits enlargement of exterior perception without interior disturbance. The Aztecs knew this, projecting images of feelings on the upper façades of buildings. Or on giant boulders at crossroads, carved to ward off evil female spirits. Sometimes overdoing the iconography with beating hearts torn fresh from living boy soldiers. Lydia smiles vaguely. Skin matte, frankly red lips as if a carefully painted mask. Taking on an air of boldness. Especially with that long American-style ciga-rette between them. Which boldness in a woman some people find annoying; others maddeningly attractive.

The two dykes look carefully around, then choose the only empty table over near the window.

Lydia watches, feeling headier and headier. Thinking: "a person, to be what she wants, just has to absorb selectively from context." Like a collector. She looks around with an air of choosing: *not* the Americans behind the line of shadow, now boasting how their troops will soon invade Iraq. But *yes* the line of rooftops, climb-ing towards the horizon; *yes* that new platinum-blonde waitress, red skintight dress, leaning over a table in a per-fect ballet stretch (the waitress's consciousness of the body causing Lydia to again raise her chin so it won't look weak, like the *mam-bo*-dancing woman's); *not* that lumpy blanket in the park, with a knee sticking out and a moth-er leaning over it; *yes* the music in this place, the plates of fish, fries, salads decorated with olives; the quite dim light; the dykes, who (she guesses) must also project themselves constantly towards the exterior, hyper-real, to forget what Mother told them, growing up.

She only wishes they wouldn't be so obvious—one has her hand on the bare, downy nape of the other. (At the bar, a guy's fist is clenched.)

This makes her feel sweaty. She sits even straighter. Enjoying herself, but wishing (briefly) it were winter. In winter, the body seems more neutral. Wearing all those clothes. Hunkering down and waiting. "Meanwhile, have a drink," says an Inuit man, sitting crosslegged in a corner of her mind. "I am," she answers fondly. "This is nothing," he continues. "In the North the winters make you feel completely stoned. Especially with that kind of rock we have up there that sings of slow, slow sunsets on the Arctic snow. Very high like whales singing." He adds: "With faulty wiring they also burned my babies." Then stood and touched her with his hairless body—

She glances at the dykes. The more obvious one (very mannish shoes) is still trying to grab, erotically, the shoulder of the other. Lydia's finger moves to the back of her collar. Where her own neck soft-as-down is getting sweatier and sweatier. But the blouse as crisp as ever to anyone observing (an old trick with starch). Noting, in the corner of her eye, that recently arrived client, watching her intently. Possibly the well-known poet "in from San Francisco" she read about in the paper. Who likes coming to this part of town "to watch the pretty shop-girls." (Which "shop-girls" think of themselves as the business-oriented women of The Main.)

She lights a cigarette (shoulders well back). Possibly he's admiring the Latinate curve of her nose. Thinking she could be Italian. Thinking he saw her, last trip, in that Italian place higher up The Main. Eating homemade pasta plus lemon ice beside an uncle. The other sisters at the table—black (instead of auburn) curls, red lips, high heels. Nervous excitement everywhere. Then a man (possibly her father) came in, a union newspaper folded in his hand. A brightly coloured television with first a soccer game, then a Roman fashion show, blinking above the door. She (who might be Lydia), getting up and going to the pool-table.

The father, reaching out to twist (in a loving way) her arm: "Listen, unemployment's terrible. The stock market totally unstable. We're really in for trouble." She, looking around and smiling, one corner of her upper lip slightly higher than the other. Standing up straighter. As if to say "fuck that, I'm feeling good. I don't want your useless fetishes. Candles, dolls, weddings. It's the 90s. People at the end of a century always have a riot."

Only the love is superfluous.

She (Lydia) hasn't had any since the boxed-in winter with the Inuit.

But her eye has strayed from the poet, distracted by a ray of purple light sweeping across the room. Tinting the bent heads of women to the colour known, on packages of hair-dye, as aubergine. She refrains from staring at the vast faded emptiness of the sky, reflected in a top-floor window across the way. With a pale sinking flame at the bottom. Calling up the Inuit again. Who was always dreaming he saw his wife's flaming face in the window of a van going down the road. The face clear, though dark, with flames all around.

"I still see my little girl running towards me. At the very same minute she was burning in one of those matchbox houses the government built up there—"

The music (a piano riff) cuts in.

She notices the dykes are staring at one another defiantly.

"Une bière," someone calls. Une Massawippi, St-Benoit, Boréale, St-Ambroise.

"Une Stella *Artois*."

They've moved their faces very close. Their profiles pale, intense, chiselled in the ever-dimming window. As if on some ancient Greek frieze. Somehow soliciting in Lydia's mind a nice pleasant image of green grass blowing in the wind (no lumpy blanket anywhere). And clouds mauve and pink. A lace curtain (like a bridal veil) blowing in a window. But what if the curtain lifts? And she (the bride) is kissing a girl in a blue camisole.

Consider light moving through lace curtains into a white room: a woman with very blonde skin is lying on a white bed. She's drunk. The thin strap of her blue camisole falls almost delicately off one shoulder, alabaster-coloured like the shoulder of some heroine of History in white stone against a blue sky. But under the tousled blonde hair in disarray on the forehead, the face's slack muscles hang in a loose grimace of despair. More like the faces of those women rubbies you used to see in the "beer-cafés" in Stockholm.

You lean over and sniff the pale nipple. Feeling angry because you've given up a radio show to be with her this night before she goes to Calgary. Why, only a week ago, on April 4, your singing body sat on the cement front steps enjoying sun and early daffodils and trying to assimilate the confusing pleasure of the night before. How put off you were when her gangly boy's body stood up and hugged you greedily in the women's bar. You hated the nervous bending of the knees, the huge feet in sawed-off cowboy boots, the faded cowboy shirt. Quickly, you retreated from her grasp.

Then as if a hand had turned, in another bar you suddenly noticed her white skin blushing slightly over high cheekbones, the elegantly curved nose: the kind you like. And her soft, pink mouth. Provocatively, you moved your shoulder close to hers and said: "How do you and your lover [she had a girlfriend in Alberta] handle sleeping with other people?" She said: "Ninety-nine point five per cent of the time I only sleep with her." You looked into your café au lait and realized how much you wanted her. Covering your desire by nodding at the moustached, smiling, confidently virile Portuguese guys leaning on the bar, while whispering from the corner of your mouth: "How're we going to make them understand we don't like pricks?" And she (to your eternal joy) answered: "Maybe like this." Grasping your head in her hands and covering your face with kisses from her mouth, sa bouche écoeurante: pink, delicious.

*Tu me fais trembler comme une feuille dans le vent avant la pluie.*

Sitting on the cement steps, writing backwards in the little Chinese book she gave you, you noticed the daffodils holding their little cups up to the darkening April sky so impatiently they also trembled. And didn't care if love produces clichés.

Yes, April is some poignant month. The snow suddenly receding in the front garden. Revealing, one by one, green shoots under last year's sludge and overgrowth. Crocuses pushing purple points through white snow. And a small bird piping, so high in a bare tree you can't see him. This time, you can, however, just barely smell the dead leaves and wet earth. Meaning your blocked senses are returning after two years of sinus problems, which makes you very sensitive. You sat in a café on April 3 and almost wept for loneliness. Outside the young choreographer passed, who wanted you last summer. He was followed by the blonde dancer. You watched him look at her with piercing eyes while she did a kind of duck walk, feet flat and somewhat apart, all the while pretending to read her newspaper.

Next your land"lord" and "lady" passed, arm 'n' arm: cool, progressive friends who had to raise the rent. Bitterly, you watched them moving as in a pas de deux, the image of the perfect couple. Pushing their offspring in a stroller, trendily dressed down, yet somehow utterly conventional. She, a dancer too, walked raising her knees as if to music, so her flared skirt drew attention to the light happiness of her gait. As if in a scene of the happy couples dancing in the movie *Oklahoma!* You always found those American musicals sexless.

Still, watching, your clitoris was a cyclops: you wanted someone, no matter how unsuitable. Thank god, only hours after mooning so desperately there in your newspaper while outside the happy couples passed, almost weeping as your nose breathed in the fumes of café au lait for comfort, she, that demi-cowgirl, was kissing you passionately in the very same bar. Love's like that. Except her kisses did not bring the sharp jab in the stomach. The tense excitement of male attention. Rather a slow diffusion getting gently warmly hotter—

It was late and she was drinking café au lait with brandy chasers, while kissing you; one mischievous blue eye cast tauntingly on the guys who were trying to flirt. Later, someone said: "You're crazy, dykes have been beat up in that place for less than that." You two just stood up, and hurried into the raw night. She, tall and blonde in her red leather jacket, with the small tight bum under the loose jeans. You rushing along beside her, shorter, darker, in brown leather. The two of you hurrying along the Grey Nuns' stone fence, where every morning (due to rising drug consumption) lay last night's crop of broken car windows.

Then, in your white room with lace curtains, she took off her cowboy shirt and turned her head as if embarrassed. You turned it back again, wanting her mouth. What a treat for one woman to have the softness of another woman's skin, to have what's usually reserved for men. You slipped the blue spaghetti straps off the shoulders. On the white bed, you ran your hands, your cheeks down the long body, so alabaster, Garbo would be jealous. Moving your lips over the pear-like mound of Venus. Her head lay sideways on the pillow, possibly in shyness. You tasted. Suddenly she lunged forward, laughing.

Still April. You step outside. The sky is so blue you sense the infinity of dancing air. Around you the jonquils are laughing. Granted, this image is slightly sentimental. You can't help it, she's getting you so drunk with the caresses of her big hands, you feel like a giant. You rock your warm crotch against the cold cement, hoping that, with all that affection, she won't be pressuring you for commitment.

The truth is, already you feel a little trapped. Because of that day she, sitting on the brown sofa in the living-room of that tacky hotel apartment she temporarily rented, knees up to chin, talking on the phone to her lover from Alberta, suddenly declared: "I'm in love, Betty." You didn't intend to listen. You couldn't believe she was putting her main relationship in jeopardy: by no means had you said anything about commitment. Yet, grudgingly, you wondered what makes these young dykes so courageous. Always taking chances. The way she kissed you in that bar, until both of you were floating. Definitely, no fear of flying.

Although sometimes you fear her forward motion, as linear as a male's, towards success and anything else she wants, might also make her cruel. Example: lying on the orange chenille bedspread in the apartment-hotel bedroom, you noticed a gigantic photo of a woman with beautiful cat's eyes emerging from a pool. You said: "Is that her?" And she answered: "Does it bother you? Okay, I'll move it." And she got up and turned the picture to the wall. But as it fell down so you could see the face again, she threw it in the closet. "There," she said. "So much for Betty." Then you were making love, but only she was coming as if in empathy while making love to you, her surprised cries filling up the air-conditioned room. After that you found yourself playing the Old Game of Love the way you used to do with men: two steps forward, one step back. So when she said: "I'm yours if you want me," lying exhausted on your chest, you said: "It's too soon for you to move here from out West. Stay there and come for visits. I'm not ready."

Then the thought of losing her kept you wet all day.

You sat in the café on The Main trying to write, afraid maybe you were pushing her off too much. While in the corner of your eye a tableau mouvant of funny people passed outside the window. The guy dressed as Superman. The crazy woman with the Walkman and long scarf attached to her wrist dancing along the street like Michael Jackson. The tough dykes in black with silver hoops from lobes to eartips. The woman from above the sign shop across the street. Who wore a different costume every day. Today, walking gracefully into the bar, head high, she was a sort of mandarin. You liked her flexibility of image. Even as a dyke, you intended to dress with a certain androgynous ambivalence.

The café door opens and an April breeze ruffles the hair on your arm. Reminding you how the thought of her sex and yours tingling side by side brings out the arrogance in you. Two white bodies. The breasts don't necessarily touch. The lips at first brush lightly, but oh so tenderly. Then it happens in the stomach. The bittersweet pain rising. The room's so quiet with the curtain of snow outside. (Even though it's April.) Women's cries are different. No my love, shh. Not yet. Breasts perking. Two pairs. Pink lips. Tongue in navel. Tongue in navel. Two times. Two wombs. The throb of blood rising full. Moon opening into concentric constellations.

You need a fix. You walk over to the phone and put a quarter in. Trying not to sound desperate.

April (near the middle). From the front steps, you sniff the damp earth. Still a little reticent. Maybe you're just having trouble trying to get adapted. Those younger dykes seem to have it easier. Possibly more centred. Also *some* of them have a terrific sense of style. Sitting in the bar-café you saw this wonderful pair go by the other day. In jodhpur pants and interesting men's shirts with collars up. Their short hair slicked behind their ears, well-cut and tinted. Watching them pass, you envied the time they had to taste the sweetness of so many—

In your case, strawberries, the little caesars, didn't bloom till later. Having once stupidly passed up a perfect opportunity in—oh bella Roma. Sitting in some trattoria late at night looking at a postcard of Bandinelli's *The Massacre of the Innocents* (a complicated tableau of every human attitude). The others at the table were lesbians from a Roman castle occupied by feminists. You could smell the odour of some melancholic blossom, maybe orange? The stone yard covered with broken glass because the fascists had attacked. Worn stone stairs rising to a room with a woman who wore a huge red flower in her hair. On the floor a long white dog with a very pointed mug. The air was electric with heat, perfume and a certain tension because through an open window, behind her strong yet delicate shoulders coming out of her red spaghetti-strapped jumpsuit, moved a temporary thunderstorm.

"Bella," she said, offering you gelato across the trattoria table. "Bella. Amore." Around you the women smiled, especially two hairy dykes from Britain, the type you can't stand. Giovanna caressed you with her beautiful brown eyes, her soft throaty voice. Speaking of a trip to Sardinia. Offering herself with a gesture of her palm. In the absence of streetlights, the stars shone above your head almost biblically. But you couldn't go with her. You were travelling north to meet a man.

You pushed back your chair (everyone was laughing). Pulling down your homemade red-flowered skirt that rides up a little on the hips. Badly cut, unlike the clothes of Roman women.

Somewhere in the dark, you smelled that flowering tree spread its perfume of regret.

However, April. And *now* you're crossing the front garden, feeling good for the first time in years. Clean shirt, pale jeans, new shortish hair. On your way to Ste-Adèle to see your new lover who's working in a sound studio up there. The sky is blue (only a cloud or two). The birds sing incredibly. And after those years of blocked sinuses that prevented you from tasting, you can smell the earth again. The grass, the garbage. Walking down the street by that turquoise building full of artists' studios you breathe the spring air deeply, so delighted to be finally taking in the sweet smells. Except just then a small fat terrier on a leash deposits a large smelly turd of greenish shit right in front of you.

Of course, in new relationships it's normal to have little reservations. They pop up unexpectedly. Example: at first you didn't mind it's *you* who has to drive to *her*. It's a pleasure driving down the highway in the fragrance of approaching spring rain. Soon you'll be together. But a storm comes up and you nearly slide off the road because on your crummy car no two tires match, making it wildly unstable. Whereas, she could have borrowed une très belle machine from the country band she's working for. To come and see you. She doesn't know how to drive, apparently on principle. "I'm post-car," she said laughing when you asked about her politics—. Yeah, post-car until she needs a lift somewhere. Example: Sunday drives, with you at the wheel, and her looking out at fields of dried-up red corn in waves against the cinder sky, jotting notes for some country song she's writing. Forgetting you're a kind of writer, too, and might want to contemplate something besides the white line down the middle. She just takes up all this space and expects others to respect it. Once when she was six, she wouldn't let her mother wear her first new dress in years. Crying, crying when the poor woman put it on, until she took it off.

"Why did you spoil things for her like that?" you asked.

"Because I couldn't recognize her in that dress."

You drive through Ste-Adèle and pull up at the studio (glass and timber in a lovely wooded area). Feeling cornered, gloomy. Until you see she's feeling lousy from a blackfly-bite reaction. Thank god it doesn't prevent the two of you from making love wonderfully well. "Spurting like little boys" (her words, not yours). After, the two of you sit in a restaurant in the village and drink good filter coffee. Hardly saying anything. The place is full of chic Québécois from the modern cottages huddled rather closely (for your taste) around the lake. Occasionally, you get invited to one of those cottages, owned by a critic. Who holds a salon there on post-modernist ideas. You love this kind of talk. In Québec, thank god, artists aren't afraid to say they're intellectuals. Your blonde lover will only speak in anecdotes. When you say to her, "Speak to me of songwriting, I mean your processes ..." she just clams up. As if the creative act involved no thinking but were totally spontaneous.

Driving back (bluish hills giving way to flat plains and the sunset of the city) you're happy the two of you live in different places. You think of writing in the little Chinese book: *Dear ———: When we've been together and I come up for air, I'm always afraid I won't be able to get back in touch with myself again. Do you feel this same schizy feeling when you step away from me into your world?*

You open up your door. The snow has nearly all receded in the front garden. You walk west towards the English part of town. Yes, you love her, with only *tiny* reservations: she speaks with an exaggerated Western drawl, like your mother, also from Alberta, did. That day you told her: "I'm broke," she, sitting on a stool in one of those trendy 50s-style bars with a pool game and a few Arborite tables in the largely empty room, replied: "Money's jiss buffalo chips." You looked round to see if anybody'd heard. The way you used to as a teenager when your mother'd drop her *G*'s on present participles in public situations. But unlike your mother, she's from the city and went to university.

You step off the dusty April street and take the Otis elevator to her apartment-hotel suite (she's back in town again). Some twangy country song about the cold war in the heterosexual couple is playing on the tape deck. You walk over and you look through the orange curtains at the sky beyond the high-rises. Thinking how that music depressed you as a kid: the sadness, no the corniness, of conventional love turned tragic. Sitting in your hot bedroom with the black maple leaves, which proliferate in villages, outside your window, hardly breathing, the thought of abandonment in love was so terrible you couldn't contemplate it. Then on the radio would come someone singing *I'm So Blue Over You (Since You've Gone)*. And you'd turn off the radio and go outside for a walk. Past your mother, in an old print dress, tending her delphiniums. Only to find the same stuff belting out the window of one of those false-fronted restaurants along the main street that made the town look like a cowboy-movie set.

Now, you look out her apartment-hotel window at the blue blue sky until you can't stand it any longer. Then you nearly scream: "Turn that tape off before you spoil everything." Because (the truth is) her stupid music is ruining your desire. Fortunately, to make it come back you know exactly what to do. Just focus on her beautiful mouth when she steps from her room. On her sexy-boy image with the free walk, hands in pockets, feet in sneakers. On how you like kissing her neck under the perfect pageboy: with her short, short bangs and shoulder-length cut, she could almost pass for a heroine from an older Hitchcock movie. The 50s look: the difference is, there's virility in her profile. And in the softness of her mouth, not a trace of weakness.

Hearing her behind you, you turn, and—. Oh no, the operative expression would be "dressed to kill." She's wearing those crepe-soled shoes like cops usually wear, and limp beige slacks, likely rayon. On top, a shirt with some tiny print, buttoned narrowly over her skinny little chest. You look pointedly at your own wide jeans, boots with square toes, shaped like those worn by schoolboys ca. 1900. And now back in fashion. Clothes that could get by in any milieu. She doesn't get the hint. The phone rings, giving you time to find a calm and balanced way to ask her to change into something moderately acceptable.

It's dusk when you finally take the Otis elevator down to the mirrored hall (she in, unfortunately, all the same clothes except the shirt, replaced, thank god, by a becoming red sweater). And step into the dusk. And she's so happy, for she's capable of losing herself in a love affair completely, that she turns a couple of times in those huge shoes, swinging her huge black briefcase, reminding you of that magic nanny in the movie *Mary Poppins* who also had boring shoes. And just had to give a swing of her black umbrella to fly over roofs.

The two of you turn east and walk towards the French part of town.

"Why do you like that music?" you suddenly ask provocatively. The two of you are climbing the slope of rue St-Denis. It's foggy enough, thank god (the weather must be getting warmer or else it's getting colder), that your French friends won't see the two of you even if they pass.

She doesn't answer. You turn and look up at her. She's walking along, breathless, her mouth wide open (she's chronically short-winded). Blue blue eyes focused on some point you can't figure out. Completely unconcerned, as usual, about appearances.

April comes, slightly later. Sitting on the front steps, you consider your reticence may be from guilt. You don't think so because you enjoy the sex so much. Of course the first time, a little hesitant. "I feel gauche," you said that night, with the light shining through the curtains, before leaning over her. This next part is harder to describe. Between the doe-like legs the slit, the flash of dusky flesh. The ribbon-like pink curled tampon-string. Above you on the pillow her head is turned to one side. Bathed in white light. Eyes closed, small smile on rosy lips. Narcissus. These young dykes think they can get away with murder.

Also if it were guilt, wouldn't you be more concerned about the neighbours? Instead, it made you smile the way the woman next door glared when she saw your blonde lover squeeze your hand over the wrought-iron fence the other day (your feet in wet spring earth). You wanted to retort: "I know girl-with-girl is sinful but at least she's Catholic." The woman has a crèche representing the ox, the ass, the shepherds, the Virgin and her baby. She won't let Protestants in for fear they'll contaminate the house.

Later, dozing on the white bed, you saw the same scene, in reverse, from your childhood. You standing on the verandah beckoning to your French friend Carmel to come on up the steps. Who just shook her head. Inside, your mother, as temporary leader of the Canadian Girls In Training, had brushed her thick chestnut hair and put on a navy-blue dress with a white collar. You stared, unable to believe it was your mother, so beautiful, reading a passage from the Bible about Salome dancing. To you and Luca N. and Candy R., sitting on the blue sofa. After which the king said Salome could have anything she wanted. And Salome said: "Okay, John the Baptist's head." Your mother put the Bible down and explained how a woman could use her charms (which were her power) to do good, or unimaginable evil.

Then the phone rang. And it was your blonde lover, saying something about Betty having cut off all contact. So the field was clear for you. The news, although it should have made you happy, caused you anguish. You fell asleep and had a dream called *El Norte*. It started off all right with a group of you getting ready for a trip at a really nice dyke's called C. There was lots of space around you, but not unfriendly. You remember thinking, "Oh, how nice to be with women." C. was sewing something that looked like a wedding ribbon (she had "une très belle machine"—those are exactly the words that come up in the dream). The ribbon, made of lace like a veil or a curtain, is to wear down her back for a play she's in about a young woman from Guatemala. The ribbon's part of an embroidered Guatemalan costume. You can feel that, for the girl, the outcome will be tragic.

Anyway, in the dream you girls all decide to hitch-hike south to a place called Bakau or something. (You don't really get the name because you don't see it in writing.) All but one are lesbian. Including B., young and brash with no sensitivity for danger, who tells someone you're—hitchhikers. You think: "It's illegal here (to hitchhike), it would have been better not to say anything." So you're standing on the roadside, afraid you'll get arrested. But B., unfazed, jumps on the side of a big truck, taking the other dykes too. Leaving only you and a straight woman named S.

The two of you go into an American roadside bar. It's grotesque with a ragged, stuffed moose over the door and two rusty pale-blue gas pumps in the front yard. As for you, the idea of hitchhiking seems more and more forbidding. You decide to stay the night in the cheap hotel next door. It has green rugs almost like Astroturf and a huge television from the 50s. This is even scarier. You decide to head home. You keep asking for the highway to the north, terrified of getting picked up by cops. You go by a huge cop station like a bunker. A whole bunch of cops comes out but disappears immediately. Then you meet some Latins. They're dancing. You dance a little too, not to blow your cover. You have on old Frye boots and a fringed cowgirl-style skirt. Also a plastic bag of belongings. The road is dirt. You're afraid to stick your thumb out because there are lots of "straight" farmhouses around. You realize you may be on the wrong road and not even know the name of the place you're going to.

You wake up kind of sweaty. In the dream analysis, Bakau becomes Dachau. However, the second association is Bar Harbor, a delicious seaside resort with long pines, the kind you like.

In the Chinese book, you write: *Sometimes, I feel like Kafka, constantly pushing people off in fear of crushing the little voice in me.*

The snow has some time ago receded in the front garden. After the clear blue sky, some clouds have come through with a whisper of rain. A thunderstorm actually, but nothing serious. The daffodils are waving in the breeze in full force. The two of you walk down the empty street, passing only the white rabbit belonging to the Jamaican shoemaker. You note how, after love with her, you walk proudly. On the heels of your feet. The reticence having transformed itself completely.

So why, in a restaurant called The Main, over scrambled eggs and coffee, do you raise the subject of her populist aesthetics? (With singer Leonard Cohen and the boxer Butch Boucher watching from the wall.) Saying that your problem with country music has to do with the women-hating notions often imbedded in the language. You think an artist should play, always, with the notion that symbols can be shifted. Deconstructed, in order to find ever new meaning. That this process naturally engenders art forms not necessarily immediately accessible to everyone—

You wait for an answer (in the next booth that famous choreographer and his perfect leading lady are eating chips and coffee). But your lover just looks, those blue eyes so brilliant you feel that, instead of taking in your words, she reflects them back on you. "Well, what did coming out, accepting your lesbianism, mean *symbolically* to you?" you ask. She looks in your dark eyes, and says nothing until she senses you a little bored, impatient. Then her two eyebrows wiggle exactly like your mother's used to when about to crack a joke:

"Uh, I don't know. I guess two cunts are better than one."

You look angrily out the window. There's L. (thank god) honking in her little red Renault. You nod goodbye and climb into the back, on the way to your women's discussion group. Admiring L.'s shoulders in a light spring dress, as she deftly manoeuvres through the traffic on the road to Verchères. And her beautiful round head which keeps turning in a passionate discussion with M.: "Mais pour nous, femmes, la représentation reste problématique," L. shouts. M. inclines her head, amused, for, in her opinion, la représentation of "woman" for lesbians implies something else entirely. Your blonde lover would never talk like that. If they ask about your romance, you'll say you and she are as different as Canada and Québec. They'll understand—but then might think it's strange that you're with her. You'll add: "A true original. Why, when travelling with her country group, she often stands in the vestibule at the back of the train shouting poems in the wind—"

The Renault winds its way past a port, old villages with the stacks of oil refineries bulging at their sides, flooded spring flats. In the distance runs the river, with a statue of Madeleine de Verchères leaning over it. The Renault veers left and stops outside a century-old house. Kittens play in the sun on the lawn. The cracked, ripe voice of a tiny woman greeting everyone. Then you're sitting around the pine table with your group. Five pairs of brown eyes (which, unlike blue eyes, reflect the Other in them). White plates of poached salmon with sauce aioli, corn, watercress salad, tourtière with homemade ketchup. The fruit salad marinated in a delicious liqueur. The silver at least a century old.

Outside the cold, wide St. Lawrence River, watched over by Madeleine de Verchères, flows deeply. Someone jokes that if Madeleine were modern, she'd be sitting here with you (instead of fighting with the Iroquois). "Pas sûr," says another. You sniff your fragrant coffee. Opening your notes: *Le lesbianisme comme déplacement symbolique.* Hesitating, because you feel the need to make a small introduction. About how you and your lover were recently sitting in a bar. "And she, though not a feminist ... said she thought two female sexes side by side function as a kind of symbolic reinforcement, making a woman feel more present in the act of love."

Right away you see your anecdotal approach is much too personal (she's influencing you already). You go faster, trying to raise the level of your discourse. "... if the phallus is the overriding patriarchal symbol—its shape or the shape of its pleasure repeated everywhere from steeples to literature to launching pads—then, when the female sex exists in double, why—." Here you stop and take a breath. Insisting on the importance of repetition; doubling; series in reinforcing ideological concepts. Of course a new symbolic order requires more than that (around the table none of the hands is writing). How you saw tension in the clenched fists of businessmen as you kissed her in the airport. That being lesbian must be privileged (in the sense of psychic reinforcement through the loving presence of one's likeness). Yet also dangerous.

"*C'est à dire, l'on passe d'une marge à l'autre—de la marge de l'hystérie à la marge de la paranoïa.*" At last they're writing.

Still, all the way home on the rain-slicked road, along the river, past the port and industrial section, towards the small street where you live, you're in a lousy mood. As if you'd exposed yourself somehow. You hate the way being with her makes you think so much in English, you lose the capacity for immediate abstraction that comes with speaking French. When you see her next, you say: "This relationship is giving me some problems."

She says: "I think it's just fine." Sitting on the front steps in a checked shirt, smiling narcissistically.

April (near the end). And the jonquils are flooding the front garden. Also, it's later in the day, but you can still smell the freshness in the air. In this weather the gay men are most flamboyant. In their purple and rust and yellow silk shirts. But you're pretty sharp too. Yesterday, sinking into the hairdresser's chair (his little black Scottie like an ornament in a sunray on the green linoleum of the kitchen), he said: "You look great, how old are you?" And you surprised yourself by answering it wasn't that but love.

Later, sipping coffee in a bar, you reminisced, deliciously. She having left on a long trip West. Oddly, the scene is that same Greek restaurant you went to the night you gave up your radio show. Where they bring you large trays of raw fish from which to choose. She's crazy about Greece. Like Leonard Cohen and his poet friends, the early-60s gang. For some reason, this strikes you as intellectually problematic. Maybe because "Greek" and "classical" often appear together, making you think of "patriarchal" and "immutable." So you asked her why she loved the place so much. She answered: "The connections between people are like those in real cowboy country."

You quelled a prick of irritation—ordering a huge plate of squid. She, taking over, ordered the largest bottle of retsina (your Québécois friends won't drink it). You kept kissing her fair cheek, showing off a little (a journalist you knew was sitting at another table). Also, you felt exalted at the space of freedom opening up before you. The squid came with moist fried potatoes (through the open window the fragrant almost biblical April night). Then baklava, swimming in its honey, plus steaming Turkish coffee. The owner offered you each a glass of ouzo (either he didn't see the kissing, or he wasn't bothered by it). She downed the whole glass and looked around for more.

Then controlled herself—by focusing on a monologue about some heroic act she'd done: how she held a guy, armed and dangerous, at bay. Singing songs on a train. There followed a long moody silence. You looked (ironically) at her huge hand on the blue-and-white tablecloth, lying protectively around her plate like a suspicious little animal. At her white neck coming out of her snap-buttoned cowboy shirt. At the photo she was giving you, legs as long as columns, standing by the Parthenon.

Later, stumbling across the park, you must have grinned at what would happen soon (behind your lace curtain). Because suddenly she said:

"I love your Edmonton smile."

This stopped you in your tracks. Nobody ever saw your mother in you like that before.

Now, sipping coffee in the bar (the April breeze blowing through the window suddenly turned to May), you think: "Maybe *any* love is nothing but illusion." As you watch, in the next booth, that famous dance troupe again eating chips and drinking beer before leaving on some tour. The choreographer and his blonde leading lady: perfect. She, androgynous in appearance. Once she even built up her muscles to look like a man and danced with a tiny (pencilled) moustache. Now she has the slimmer body of a ballerina, which comes almost willow-like out of her loose scooped white top (with some leotard under) and the loose khaki pants over chunky shoes. The way she can change really shows you what technology can do. As if the body were machinery.

The dancer raises her mug to toast her choreographer. Even though he, dressed in loose clothes like hers, albeit all in black, seems to be flirting with someone else. One of the younger members of the troupe, perhaps, whom he's kissing. But the blonde dancer has a complicit twinkle in her eye. She gets up to phone. He follows and, while she's talking, tweaks her little nose. After which they embrace sweetly, naively, as if their love were three days' old. You wonder if this is a true reflection of their feelings, given they've known each other for years. Or if a show for the attendant audience (everyone is watching them).

You write in the Chinese book (moving from back to front): *Dear ——: Can one woman be every (any) thing to another? Is this real? Are we real?*

In the next booth the blonde dancer stands up and puts on a thick, squarely cut man's jacket over her thin clothes. You drink in every detail of her dress from the shoes, also fairly thick, to the way the tweedy lapels of the coat are folded forward over her thin neck, above which thin strands of blonde hair escape from her ponytail. Clearly, an aesthetic involved in integrating life and the process of creation until every gesture, every move tends towards a new sense of beauty—the ultimate of which is a criticism of culture.

You lean back, pleased with this analysis. Surveying the murmuring café, head raised, in a profile you believe attractive: brown curls; a chin, well-defined, but which still occasionally wiggles somewhat insecurely; the nose not quite turned up in an American snub, thank god. On the TV, a singer from Alberta (your lover idolizes her) is singing *Watch Your Step Polka*. You think: "Why, it's country music—deconstructed." Then the singer flies through the air, one leg out behind. Just like your blonde lover, once, to show her joy on seeing you after Ste-Adèle (landing flat out at your feet).

Maybe there's something about these Western women you haven't understood—

Rapidly, you turn the pages of the Chinese book: *Dear ——: Since you left, I only think of you. After all the rain, the sky is washed clean and blue. You give me light. You give me courage. Yes you*

Somewhere, out there, she looks up. Her twinkling eyes as blue as the high blue sky outside the window, earlier. And getting bluer as you watch.

**(the sky is what I want)**

Outside the window, the sun has sunk to the point of turning shadows cinder.

In the bar a piano riff: things heating up for the moment, imminent, when the sky, colourless as chalk, suddenly turns to dark. Clients pouring in. Standing or sitting under ledges tacked high on the wall, with stuffed real little animals on them. Although the plants hanging from the roof are fake. Clinking of glasses and loud conversation. The light, a pénombre almost, levelling the tops of heads, all the rest etched darker.

Lydia looks in her purse. Small, black, with Guatemalan embroidery. And removes a tube of lipstick. Thinking: "not as bad as expected." Meaning this empty stretch of day when time seems to stop for a second (something like eclipses). When beer is sold two-for-one to cheer people up. Making them loquacious.

She smiles, half-ironically. Even enjoying the last fil-tered rays dusting the tops of cornices, parapets, turrets, and every other object inside the bar and out. Reminding her of a play of light she once saw in the park (*not* that scene this morning, with a damned fake-cheerful mother by a lumpy blanket): how, after rain, the setting sun had washed the north-west half of tree-trunks, grass blades, glass skyscrapers beyond the Grey Nuns' fence, plus every-thing that moved, in gold. So that walking there, each step was through gold's shadow, the darkening grey-brown of night on the south-east side of trunks. Except she knew her back, elbows, hair, were illuminated like the north-west side of the trunks in a wash of yellow-silver light. And people moving through this stunning contrast of light and dark (entirely muting the blues, greens, greys, browns of the park) felt, no matter what their stride, that they were tiptoeing towards the future.

She thought of this as "memory's motor" without knowing why.

With her dimpled lip, she smiles. Liking how the music in the bar's increasingly sensual, insistent. Covering that voice somewhere saying: "I can't wear men's pyjamas, they remind me of my father." Her head cocked, consid-ering one more to stay afloat. Thinking again of winter. When time's imperceptible drift towards dark and back again in layers of white, palest blue, grey, is hypnotic in itself. When nothing happens. Except days of sexual play-ing in the white light of the room. The unusual lover's finger helping you taste your vaginal juices. Time of sensation being time in suspension. Unlike time stopped (death). Or time of understanding, which time is linear: which passes. Except for Guilt of History: the Guilt of dogs shot dead by Mounties, so the people couldn't hunt. Of sequestered children in camps called "residential schools." She wanted him to punish her so much she did the opposite. Locking him out of her room (high ceilings, chipped mouldings, fake fireplace, dun-coloured rug).

At dusk he crashed through the window.

Anyway (outside the sky nearly charcoal), *now* she's feeling as good as she looks. Her lovely profile (fresh plum lipstick, mole high on cheek) in the window. Leaning forward, tapping to her own internal rhythm. As tropes of various possibilities walk down the street. A woman in white cowboy shirt with black embroidery on it. White jeans, belt around the waist. Over-large earrings. A dusky queen, in red, head twisting hard over one shoulder to the beat of his Walkman. A smooth refugee leaning on a car selling illicit cigarettes (the only job available). Music. A voice saying *"à chaque fois que je passe par là j'ai une lueur d'espoir ..."*

The music (jazzy piano) stops for a second.

She rapidly lights a cigarette. Thinking that the problem with feeling better (calmer) is, it opens space for the inner anguish under. Listening, in the rests of the music (playing even louder), for that voice saying *"par là, une lueur d'espoir."* Fresh (she speculates) from walking on rue Viger, a vista she loves: deserted stone buildings, empty factories, narrow empty streets. Fake owl on the

edge of a parapet to scare away the pigeons. Lydia loves
that image. Loves to think architecturally (as part of her
new take on History), once the sun's gone down. Different
ways of light on pediments in different parts of town. In
the better French parts, the gracious greystones, façades all
symmetrical, yet forming different patterns (reminiscent
of New Orleans). Or, in this mixed neighbourhood, a
tackier mix of brick, stone, tin, sagging awnings, half-suns,
fleurs-de-lys, little Aladdin lamps on tiny turrets, designs
ordered from American architectural catalogues at the turn
of the century. Just now the last thin spit of light casting
relief on the edges, the whole becoming fantastical and
mysterious. Making her think of the Aztecs, whose tem-
ples crystallized the universe. Using surreal-looking reliefs,
plus costumes, feasts, parades, to attenuate the harshness
of their vision: History's perpetual turning on itself to the
point of annihilation.

"Unfortunately," she thinks, "we doom-say as much
as they." Suddenly feeling certain—though she couldn't
say why—that she is on the verge of an alternative. That
circumstance (her place in the century), plus her sex are
combining at this very moment, just below the surface, in
some extraordinary vision (if she could just put her finger
on it). Something so original, it could shake Western
thinking—

"*Un carafon,*" she calls, elated. Considering squid, as
well, marinated in vinaigrette, with lots of little chopped
peppers of various colours on them (to get herself in shape
for the task at hand). Trying not to mind that the bar
door opens, revealing two cops, exactly like the ones by

that lumpy blanket earlier today. "Totally insignificant," she says firmly to herself. Barely refraining (the regulars are watching) from getting up and dancing beside her table. Hips moving expertly in the short, tight skirt to the Etta James blues playing on the tape deck.

Instead—she lights a cigarette. Eye fixed obliquely on the Portuguese woman, *herself* jumping up, despite the heat, to put some quarters in the parking meter. Or is it cooling off? Lydia makes a fan from her placemat. Adoring how those in this bar from Latin cultures, particularly, usher in the pleasures of the night. Although, it's true, her eye (traced with a curved line of black, particularly decisive at the outer corner like on a Greek frieze, indicating the strain of Mediterranean in her) in looking round can't help noticing that everybody, regardless of their language (English, French, Portuguese), is eating *moules, sauce piquante, frites,* washed down with many pitchers of local draft beer.

"I mean," she thinks, "pleasure with a Latin sense of ritual. Suggestion and deferral." As in that French-speaking woman with pretty long curls, leaning forward (perfectly straight back) hour after hour, in anticipation. Her guy, still stretching like a cat. Or the woman outside on the street, just before the sun took its final dip below the horizon. Whose cherry hair matched her cherry shoes. The two almost on fire in the last cherry light glazing the windows running up the street. An omen of sensations reassuring Lydia she's reached the real state of detachment, when one finally becomes a person. Free enough to take in all exterior impressions. She hums her song of somnambulence:

*C'est quand tu dors*
*Que je t'appartiens*
*Par la fenêtre*
*Je t'observe.*

The woman dressed like a mandarin, who's just come in again (despite *saying*, earlier, she would take a bus to Ottawa), climbs on a barstool. Her little hat, flat, round, embroidered, perched jauntily on her curls. Lydia likes this attention to dress. "Hats," she thinks, "are like architectural details, often pointing somewhere." In this case, the peasant or natural look for periods when, politically, people are exhibiting sympathy for the oppressed. Then, time slips (so easily) beyond sympathy for small cuddly animals and: real fur again. Little fur earflaps tied behind a woman's head, revealing a glistening burnished-red ponytail. Quite provocative. Her own last hat (crushed in the blue metal trunk at the end of her bed) reflecting, like her black skirt and white blouse, the end of a period of fashion-devotion to business. A little royal-blue felt number she wore on her crown. Leaving her freezing ears exposed as she walked along rue Mont-Royal towards a women's gallery. Having said goodbye, *Tagvauvutit,* pointedly to the Inuit. Then seeking other distant but friendly contacts (even a woman who's chosen to be alone has to talk a little). Opening the gallery door, she liked the way those gallery women looked, different shades and cuts of hair against the white walls. They even surprised Lydia with their response when she reached out to them. Reaching out to her—

But friends (like time) slip off.

Lydia stands up carefully (on her way to pee). Distributing lipstick, lighter, Kleenex on her table so no one else will grab it. Eye, for ballast, now on those two dykes still staring defiantly at each other, pretending love is everything. She sits down again. Because the waitress, slightly double chin despite her perfect carriage, seems *at last* headed for her table. She makes her small, discreet order: espresso (instead of wine), with, yes, a brandy chaser. The door opening, again, on a group of failed artists (the successful ones are working). Coming to grab a bite. Before going to drink "fabulous local beer" in another neighbourhood.

"By the way, what happened to your face?" one of them says, loudly, to his friend.

"Herpes?"

Lydia looks out now unable to see the sky. "You looked so good lying there, with your cigarette, and him on top of you," says a female voice behind. "The cops got me hooked so I could work for them," says a second, high, defensive. "You bitch," says a third (the scraping of a chair). She sips some brandy, thinking, "this tension must be due to the fullness of the moon." Wishing (momentarily) she could go back to six p.m. again. When the bright, clean sunlight still cut across the bar, slicing water-beaded glass, half-baguette, and carafon in two. Which carafon she had downed too rapidly. Feeling a terrible restlessness of the body. Having fled the park; having lain carefully down in the nuns' garden beneath the fragrant branches (kind of blacking out). Later, hurrying down Coloniale to the steambaths (unfortunately closed to women every day but Tuesday). Back along the summer sidewalk. A lazy leg and yellow dog hanging from the second-storey window of the student restaurant. That mother's fake-cheerful voice by the lumpy blanket following in her mind. Saying (defensively) to the cops: "My daughter just called the other day.

"'Hi Mom,' she said, the way she always does."

On second thought, now the line of shadow has completely engulfed the room, it's easier to (unobtrusively) relax. She slowly sips her brandy. Watching, from the dark neutrality of her corner, the regulars still at the bar: the writer's briefcase by the video machine, fallen down and dirty; Ralph, exiting from the can, obsessive medals bouncing; a Québécois guy (small goatee, glasses), always speaking French, but "listening" in English. Farther down the counter, that poet from San Francisco. Gazing at her, intently. As if waiting for an answer.

Unless he's looking by her—

"It's true," she thinks, sipping: "a person can be overly self-conscious if sole and all alone." The word "sole" recalling some thread from earlier this evening—at the point when the woman dressed as a mandarin came in the first time. Having stepped elegantly across the hot summer street. Lydia, sure she knew her. A woman (first spied at the gallery) who, the worse she felt inside, the better she was able to project a large and confident image. But, today, Lydia didn't talk to her (now she rarely talks to anyone). Preferring to save her energies for the task before her: imagining a new kind of History, open, floating, like a field of flowers. Instead of rigid, even homicidal—

"I know I fucked up by failing to admire his stew

"With the seven bay leaves in it," says another voice somewhere.

Not a candidate for her "brides" on the roof. Lydia lines up her portraits for perusal: Nanette (cute and smart), the woman from Halifax (a little crazy, maybe, but following her *élan*), the *mam-bo*-dancing woman (Lydia can't forget the knife in her boot), the two dykes, now getting up to leave (the taller one is paying). Searching out the window for the proper setting for them, the right collection of little roof-trim details to enhance their party: a Louis XVI grille, orbs on the corners of a parapet, a dome-shaped gable covered with blue-scalloped shingles, carved brackets holding up a cornice over a frieze of rosettes.

But again Lydia feels nostalgic for that point, earlier, when that woman dressed like a mandarin came in the first time. Clothes and makeup a little paler now, on account of the heat. A woman in some ways impossible to grasp (unless it was Lydia who backed off). Always appearing in ambivalent and parsimonious fragments. As if precariously constructed in both the official (French) and unofficial (English) language. So the English in her at war against the French—and the reverse. Only when confident (self-absorbed) to the point of neutral could the woman synthesize the two. Becoming extraordinary.

Lydia looks out. The bar is growing quieter. Remembering she *did* speak to someone today. Some ... coincidence from her past: an unemployed architectural historian she knew (before the boxed-in winter). Who, on opening the door of the bar (the sun still fairly bright in the sky), came directly to her table.

Then stood there, restlessly, as if he'd made an error.

"What's that?" she'd asked quickly, conversationally, pointing out the window.

## Z. Who Lives Over The Sign Shop

"What d'you call that thing?

"A pe——?"

"A pediment," he answers.

The tall thin man with elegant clothes and long grey hair tucked behind his ears laughs and walks away.

Lydia laughs too. With an air (to cover her embarrassment) of someone from a Simone de Beauvoir novel (black-and-white outfit, head back a little). Albeit, slightly English accent when speaking French. That tense *almost* voyeuristic tint to her gaze. Now straying across the street again. The building has three storeys. Tacked to its top, where its stone façade meets its flat roof, that high piece of ornamental metal, painted ochre. A fake pediment— because no depth. Running the building's width, with scrolled peak and the year 1904 written uncertainly in the middle, it leans slightly back upon the wide blue late-afternoon sky as if to brace itself against the weather. From there, a line of other flat-topped roofs reaches down the street and curves around the corner under an azure ceiling with intermittent clouds. Reminiscent, in its way, of New Orleans.

Lydia's eye shifts down the building's front. Each storey, with its quatuor of large square windows, seems to serve a different purpose. She gazes up once more to a large apartment window on the building's top floor. From the foliage in it, a plastic pink flamingo delicately sticks its neck out. Beneath, on the second floor, a sign shop. Its windows all blocked out with notices reading SIGNS/ENSEIGNES (VENTE, BARGAINS, RABAIS). The first floor's banal, commercial: a cheap clothing store with crooked awning. In a partly open door beside it, a woman. Lydia, giving a blink of recognition. Having seen that face somewhere—

A face that wanted love, that was certain. Sitting in some restaurant on The Main. With white skin (the kind that, growing up, had the right kinds of vitamins). And hennaed hair. Almost a travesty of self: half flower—that withdrew. If you scratched it with a slightly pointed nail. Half clown. Sweeping her brightly coloured vestments through the town. Hair purple-red. Dewy, well-shaped forehead. Wrist protectors. Colour deflectors. Striped leg-warmers. And the elusiveness of her gaze! An incredible clear colour of turquoise that melted away when you asked for information. The same eyes in all the faces of her various incarnations. Female junkie. *Vogue* model. Pisces woman. Aging punk. The physical beauty of each. And the secrets that went with them. "How do you pay for your habit?" someone asked her once. The answer: silence. The turquoise eyes reproachful before melting into absence. Briefly, as New Wave Artist, Z. gave performances of astonishing black humour. Once, coming down the aisle in clown's white, balancing Pierrot-like on one foot with the other polka-dot leg sticking out in front, she pointed to the leg and said, half-sheepishly, half-mocking:

"This is my e-rection."

Now she comes out of the building across the street, dressed as a kind of mandarin. A pale version of how she used to be. In toned-down colours, hair less mauve than russet, piled elegantly on her head. Makeup perfect, yet almost imperceptibly applied. Spotless high collar, wide linen pants. Followed by a small Caucasian man with a pigtail down his back. They turn right and step along the sidewalk, her arm around his slender waist, towards the health-food store. As if they lived a perfectly ordered life. Then back again, and through the bar door. Sitting at a table. Except, the restless male gets up and leaves quite quickly. Hardly saying anything. She, watching him. The pale line of her cheek, with the powder pretty well concealing a slight loosening of the skin. Apparently untroubled by his action. As if the departure of a lover could only be incidental, so great the pain was elsewhere.

"How do you pay for your habit?" the acquaintance had persisted. Angry at the elusiveness in Z.'s gaze. (*In the dream, Z.'s walking away. A boarded-up house. You're robbed. Her indifference [the junkie connection]. But it doesn't frighten you.*) Finally the acquaintance (Lydia, to tell the truth), having heard rumours, said the ultimate to be vengeful: "Feminism would help you ground yourself. Uh, help you stop living with guys who chase you with stud-ded belts." Z.'s voice, almost expressionless:

"Je te crois un peu ja-louse de mes amants."

Lydia watches patiently. Across the street, the door blows slightly open. Revealing only wooden stairs climbing to the redhead's flat. Some sign-shop men descend carry-ing a ladder. They march down the street, turn, march back again, the ladder held between them. They're carry-ing a sign. For a moment in the bar, in a space between songs on the tape deck, there is silence in which Lydia feels the anguish of suspension in the coming heat of sum-mer. Especially without love. Or with it if one has fear of losing. "Qu'il fait chaud!" says the redhead. Asking the waitress for orange juice.

Lydia glances at the window across the street. With the pink flamingo, now leaning back, slightly. Wondering, retrospectively, if it's the window of her bedroom. The dresser in it with, no doubt, rounded corners, stained dark, 50s-style. On which sit all the pots that keep her beautiful. The small wooden stick to put on kohl. The envelope of henna for her hair. Some jewellery. The room smelling vaguely of her perfume. Light shines across the floor and off the convex mirror. The window's closed, but you can hear the traffic in the street. The room may also carry, like many empty rooms, the echo of its owner's voice: its flatness. Revealing (when speaking English) not a trace of native French.

Unless the flatness itself is a sign of what lies under it.

Oddly, on the phone, that same flat voice came through rich, erotic. As if the self were best projected through technology. A voice (before Lydia had actually met its owner in the flesh) magnetized by telephone wires. Conjuring up in the mind an image of white rooms, with low bed on which to stretch one's body. A kitchen with a beautiful earthy woman, and fragrant coffee dripping into a nice ceramic pot. The whole scene radiating the sensuality of a house that's clean, with drawers all neatly ordered, scented, perhaps, with blossoms, windows gleaming, bedclothes fresh, unwrinkled. And the tray, when deposited (by the still-imagined Z.: ample breasts and flowing skirt) near the bed that she, Lydia, was lolling on, would have a small vase of dried blue flowers on it.

Except, in person, Z. had turned out to be a kind of emaciated drag queen. Appearing at a women's exhibition in the museum all dressed in black. Lace gloves cut off knuckle-length. She lifted one such gloved hand and twirled her fingers in the curls of a woman standing there. Then disappeared into the crowd (breaking the woman's heart), ephemeral, with that sheepish, almost boyish smile.

Not before saying to the woman:

"I'm in lo-ove."

And Lydia inquiring: "Man or woman?"

Across the street, the leaning-back flamingo in the window, under the round corner of the flat roof and sky, makes her think (again) of New Orleans. Where, similar to this place, long balconies deck the backs of courtyards. Then (incongruously) an image of a piece of crumpled paper flying down the sidewalk here, on The Main. Past a café where she and Z. went occasionally, before High Art invaded. Full of ordinary crazy people, speaking French and English. Although French definitely in the ascendant. Water dripping, when it rained, through the roof. Lydia sitting there with Z., sated by her presence. Despite the tension due to her (Lydia's) saying feminism was the antidote to studded belts. Silence—. Z., finally, showing by speaking first she still cared enough to close the gap that had opened up between them. Her voice, as usual, flat:

"I don't like ism's. I'm an artist."

Lydia brushing back a lock, waiting.

A little drip of water fell beside the table. A gay man sitting near them smiled brightly. Outside, that ball of crumpled paper was lodged against the wall. Lydia waited, still having the confidence of the beginning of a relationship: that is, power. Z. again reached out. Her flat voice rising somewhat on certain syllables to get in a complimentary note (which note, Lydia thought hopefully, she only used for courting):

"This scarf accent-uates your cheekbones."

Now, across the bar, the redhead neatly folds a hanky. Is she really Z.? She has the same savoir-vivre: looking crisp while everyone else is hot. Z. was in her element in summer. Nobody wore a sleeveless dress like she did: nipped-in waist, bare golden shoulders emerging from some bright mid-century print (everything she bought was second-hand). The epitome of the urban woman on a summer sidewalk. (Hot wind blowing.) Or stepping in yellow print from a shop into the street's glare, holding tapes of Etta James: *The Blues Don't Care*. The down that grew copiously on her arms (since she started living cleaner) dancing a reflection in the summer light.

"What's up?" Lydia had asked, gluttonous, embarrassed.

The redhead sitting across the bar says: "Qu'il fait chaud. J'attends ici le bus pour Ottawa." Serene, yet disciplined. Jaw held firmly at an angle so as not to betray the looseness of the flesh. Z., also from Ottawa, was skinny. But sometimes, when laughing, her jaw hung a little loose due to drinking beer and brandy (no ice, even in the heat). Otherwise, perfect in every manner. Back so straight the shoulder blades, in the scoop-necked summer clothes, practically disappeared. Or, the time Lydia spied her at the Bains Coloniale, where women went in winter for massage and Turkish bath: impeccable woollen underwear. Long straight neck. Z. hated sloppiness of any sort. She feared (being bilingual from growing up in that English-dominant city) that speaking English caused slackening of the mouth. French being in every way clearer, more precise. Was it the transparency of French (which English pretends to have, but doesn't) that made her keep her life so secret?

Lydia blinks again. Seeing another ball of paper blow down a sidewalk—in New Orleans. (The association could be the heat.) Reminiscing, not about New Orleans, where careening voices in the street mingled with the odours of Cajun food and heat. But about bygone cafés on The Main, where patrons (before the phonier, safer decadence of gentrification set in) would stop their prattling and stare when Z. appeared. Taking in the beauty of her various personae. Banal yet mysterious. Worn like masks against the dark architecture of a summer night.

She gets an image of Z. sitting on some outside steps. With red lips slightly smiling, striped top, nipped-in waist—like the female lead in a French New Wave film. Hanging straightbacked, obsequiously onto a small, wired poet. Fawning over him (as if she cared). Behind them in a building—synthesizers blasting. While a male performer in black pants, white shirt, chin angled like a slide rule, moved across a stage cutting the contracted, geometric figures of the 80s. A show called *Business.* "It's fa-bulous," said Z. "I'm totally dis-illusioned—," meaning she could never reproduce, with her spare-yet-softer female body, those angles in a performance of her own. Lydia (silently) reproached her for wanting to. Tired of her charades. Z. reduced everything to theatre. Refusing to use political discernment regarding images. Invoking goddesses instead of sisters—

True, she understood the effectiveness of certain art before the critics did.

Also, Z. was perfect as Pierrot. In a kneelength white jumpsuit (patterned stockings under) for her performance called *Dys-sexion.* Building obelisks on stage, from found materials, to use for fucking. (On a video screen an endless stream of female ejaculation.) But every time Pierrot mounted one, legs apart, like a woman, the construction tumbled. Leaving Pierrot in a pile of debris, smiling sheepishly. Slowly stripping to become a woman dressed in sequined green. Matching fingerless gloves. Standing, vulnerable, on a grey-and-white sidewalk in some metropolis. Then half-nude (although she conspired never to show her breasts), circling the room. On the video screen the body represented as androgynous, bilingual: two halves placed atop a cross. Z. coming down the aisle with that rare, love-me smile creeping up her face. Brightening the skin, the dimples, the mischief in the gaze. Lydia looks across the bar in search of similarities.

The redhead's coolly reading. As if not even waiting for her small, oriental-looking Caucasian lover to come back again. So pale, light, compared to the bright, outrageously coloured images of her past. As if to weed out chaos: the pale exterior perhaps permitting a smoother flow of energy. Neither walled up nor leaking wildly out. Yet this self so airy, a touch might make it fly away. The surface of a story (or stories) that wind deeper in the silence. Like that ball of crumpled paper blowing on the sidewalk. Opening it, you'd get some traces of her—if you could catch it.

*Sometimes* (in the past) Z. would appear calm, like the redhead. Example: entering the bar dressed up as guru. Lydia could *really* drink this in: Z. as nurturer. Hair combed back. In loose white clothes after yoga lessons. Total fasting was her means of metamorphosis (for the trip back from coke). Lydia imagines a room on rue Mentana. A pink dawn roof on which a woman's rolled in a blanket. Watching the brightening of the gas station down below, the park. The skyscrapers of the city. Getting up to work (the day she stopped). Did an explosion of the mind precede the trip to empty "normalcy"? The therapies, the exercise, ointments, purges. Even exorcism. Nobody knew as much about the body. So that at a New Year's party (right at the beginning), when she, Lydia, suddenly went pale and started shivering, Z. jumped up and made her miso soup, which warmed her up immediately. But later, when she, Lydia, grew round, her purple clothes straining, her hair limp and hanging in her face, Z. refused to aid her in self-improvement:

"There's no point. Un-til you dry out."

"She overdid the therapies" (Lydia thinks, meanly). Nobody did as many. Until so focused on the Self, so contained—instead of dispersed, fragmented like before —that she no longer blended in with the moving fore-ground of the street, passing by continually: an endless parade of fashion-conscious people, hyper-sensitive to the ambience around them. Instead, like a fixed point of light, so concentrated, she couldn't see past her boundaries. So restrained ... Z. even gave up the notion of previous incarnations. On this point, Lydia finds the redhead's mandarin allure (perhaps recalling a dead Chinese ances-tor) somewhat reassuring. Because, although, she, Lydia, was anti-esoteric, she found it interesting for a basis of dis-cussion that Z. (in the past) believed she carried her earlier lives with her. "What's nostalgic is reactionary," Lydia had said provocatively to Z. Hoping to start a friendly little argument. But she never managed to get Z. cornered in any dialogue about these issues. Attempts at serious con-versation only made Z.'s turquoise gaze shift restlessly, noncommittally. Carefully drawing energy from the air as if only the energy of the moment could hold the frag-mented self together.

Fortunately, for a while (at least—Lydia *thought*), she and Z. were tight. Meeting often in that dilapidated café: almost getting personal. Z. talking about a move. To rid herself of lovers: small wired poets who solicited boys in the park. She called them her obsessions. Z. was always moving. Sitting on the front steps in the sun. While boxes, carried by her fans, full of throws, shawls, pillows, records, were passed and loaded on a truck. Anyway, after not seeing Lydia for quite a while, Z. took off her coat in the dilapidated café, to show a black turtleneck, a waist so tiny in its wide belt, that Lydia held her breath, fearing she was starving. Z. said, her flat voice registering below the café's tinkling jazz:

"When I don't have lo-ove, I'm so unhappy. I literally don't know where to put my bo-dy.

"Mais quand j'en ai, c'est insup-portable."

Lydia had felt a tightening of the throat. Pausing, after that, in the treed street outside Z.'s latest flat. Leaning on her bicycle. Looking up at curtains with blood-red birds blowing in the purple frame of the window. Wondering what Z. wore. Maybe a loose black top and crushed-velvet tights. Pulled on for breakfast following long waiting hours in a sepia-coloured room. Paint was peeling off an outside door. Finally, love at dawn, with pink sun rising over tree-tops, flat roofs, telephone wires outside the window. And the other (no one could say who) having left, Z. sat at her table. Drinking a certain tea to eliminate the excesses of the night before. She had to.

Z. had also appeared (once) as lesbian. This was the nearest Lydia got to intimacy with her: a car driving to the country. Lydia beside her, taking in that odour of herbal bath-salts she found maddeningly seductive.

Inching closer. Z. dressed uncharacteristically simply: black pedal-pushers and sleeveless white shirt. A dangling daisy earring. Then standing on a brilliant summer beach in a faded leotard-for-bathing-suit (the black worn down to purple). Staring at the thick hair growing on her legs: "Je fais des progrès en tant que les-bienne. I'm lear-ning not to shave." A mocking sadness emanating from her golden body. Z.'s lover (not Lydia, who only watched) throwing a rubber raft upon the waves. Then ruffle, ruffle over water. Two women in a raft and their legs touch, and fingers. Twinkling. Twinkling. Shoreward. Two women with a raft coming up the sand. Small waves, damp feet, a blue sky like her beautiful lover's eyes. Z. happy, yet also sad. Although the women's fingers still touched putting the raft of rubber in the trunk. And the blue car and the raft of rubber were going down the road. And beautiful Etta James, deep blues voice of desire, flooding up the car. Outside, the golden dusk, muted beautifully in grey, streaks off the mountains. Then the car stops at wooden steps pattering down to water. Another lake: now in darkness, so a threatening pool. Z.'s voice quivering in the night:

"Eh, les girls, il faut ren-trer. Unless we're going to New Or-leans."

Lydia surveys (more critically) the building across the street. Its flat-topped wide-skyed air of New Orleans. A place (like Montréal) attracting people who've failed to be a hit in their own language. But in the bright, late June afternoon, the building's tacky: old, slightly crooked aluminum windows, behind which, strips of fluorescent lighting. Pock-marked stone front, tattered awning, old signs covering the window of the second floor. In New Orleans (Lydia in love and losing), the façades were cleaner, more classic French. The wrought-iron balconies circling the backs of buildings even longer (like tiers on Mississippi river-boats) than balconies here. Lydia, sitting in the hotel garden there, looked up and saw hard-edged clouds over flat flat rooftops. As in a set for a movie. So hot, she was glad the rooms were dark. The hotel proprietress behind her big fan in the fern-filled lobby. Saying slowly, the better to keep cool: "Y'all c'ld have a-ny room ya wanted" (Lydia was travelling with a man).

All of them were empty! But the beds were huge and damp. Covered with darkly patterned spreads and worn rugs: perhaps a former brothel. Lydia and her partner sank into one, fucking deeply (ignoring the dangers inherent in the lesions on the penis). The jazz floating sweetly on the hot night air. He the much-desired one and she so thin in the cavity of her chest. Hunched over, listening to the silence grow between them. Later, in a bar, despite the magnificence of her curls, her tense back showed anguish at being only able to raise conversation on the failing merits of the couple. Which didn't prevent her from noticing a Cajun woman speak authoritatively in French to the waiter (whether he understood or not). While her man hung behind. Outside, a crumpled ball of paper rolling down the sidewalk. Past a bumper sticker which lamented: ICI PERSONNE NE PARLE FRANÇAIS.

Back in Montréal (the man withdrawing), Lydia had naturally called Z. immediately. They went and sat in that dilapidated café. It was then that Lydia held her breath as

Z. took off her coat. Noting the increasing thinness of Z.'s waist and wondering again: was it speaking mostly English when she was French that made Z. distant yet vulnerable? Always tracing a crooked line from the French-thinking body to the English-speaking words. Strange, Z. placed the emphasis on English when she didn't have to. "It's all theatre, darling," said the gay man at the next table to no one in particular. Brushing back her lock, Lydia said (this time kindly) that, *really*, feminism would help Z. synthesize her differences. So she wouldn't be a victim.

"What makes you think I am?" Z. answered coldly.

"You're the vic-tim: always trying to mo-ther."

Across the street, now, the door leading to the red-head's flat (and the sign shop under it) swings slightly open. The sign-shop men, dressed in white, march past again. The problem being how to place their sign, which says ENSEIGNES SIMON, in conformity with the French-only sign law, over the one which says SIMON'S SIGNS in English, Arabic, Hebrew. Given the new one is inadequate in size to cover the Arabic script, the Hebrew lettering, plus of course the English (writ large) of the old. A huge crash makes Lydia turn her head. Simon, the sign-shop owner, has dropped his plate. While changing tables the better to see the operation. Simon says:

"I'm sha-king."

The waitress (not French) brings another, leaning over kindly.

He doesn't touch it: only drinks more and more. Shaking violently. Lydia thinks: "clearly a liver problem—angry bile." So how does he still his hand to paint the big

white letters with rounded corners on the bright red sign-
boards in his shop? Simon says:

"Delir-ium tre-mens.

"Or else nerves from this French *on-ly* law."

Lydia sits, eyelids half-drooping in the heat. Dis-
gusted with Simon's lack of understanding that language
needs power to survive. Noting vaguely that the pink
flamingo in the third-floor window seems to have
changed direction. Leaning back. Conjuring, with its pink
tail-feathers jutting to the left, a woman in a fuchsia summer dress. All elastic. On a corner of a street. If over 35,
only a woman eating rice exclusively could dress like that.
Z. ate rice. Her philosophy in clothes was similar: no
additives, no rayon, polyester. Only silk, cotton, wool,
excellently maintained. Nobody knew like she how to
coax into shape the things she skimmed from bazaars and
garbage. To make tomorrow's fashions. (Except that horrid négligé with fur trim she found behind the fish store.)

Lydia's eyes open, distracted by a sunray from the
street, piercing the bar window. Cruelly casting light on
the puffiness of the redhead's face. A face that was once so
gaunt! Unless it isn't her. For this woman's so serene. It
occurs to Lydia (with a certain satisfaction) as the redhead
raises her thumbnail to smooth her brow, that Z.'s effort
to achieve an almost perfect surface may have spoiled her
black humour: Z. coming down the aisle in some performance, balancing on one foot. Half-sheepish. Then suddenly sticking out the leg to face you. In striped leotards,
as if to say:

"Keep your dis-tance."

Lydia knew the need for distance. Having been, herself, one of those people you meet travelling. Who feels better in another language. Spending hours in her room dressing up "to pass." People also accused *her* of remoteness, except, when lonely or wanting something badly—

"You mo-ther to control. Also, you're cha-sing me," Z. had added that time in the dilapidated café. Lydia was stunned. A "mo-ther"—when she, Lydia, was radical and cool! (Silently) she mocked Z. for being "superficial": refusing (for example) all political discussions. Claiming (to be mean) that her performances were a piling up of images lacking social context. Making a point about her own empathy with the struggles of people on the street, Lydia gestured out the window. At a kid eating rabidly from a garbage can outside. Z. shrugged. (*You're robbed. Her indifference [the junkie connection]. But it doesn't frighten you.*) As if Lydia were waxing sentimental. Who, to deflect this stab of disappointment, just focused on Z.'s flat voice coming from the hollow in her chest. Clearly, thought Lydia, Z. needed love, nurturing. What irony, considering that in the first place (the beginning of the relationship), nurturing was what she, Lydia, had hoped to get from Z.

Across the street, the door to the wooden stairs blows back again.

Lydia thinks: "maybe those stairs do not belong to her." Because who would have turned the pink flamingo round so now its neck is in the foliage and its tail dipping backwards over the planter's edge. Instead of the neck reaching delicately outward as it did before? Given *she's* sitting here in the bar? Clearly not caring that the Caucasian oriental-looking man left abruptly, and hasn't come back again. Of course, this serenity could be one of her charades: Z. standing "homeless" with a hatbox on the sidewalk. Or Z. lying, majestic, in her faded leotard on the burned grass of the park. The white clouds in the sky making her fear rain. Insensitive to the fact the world is drying up. Saying, in a voice made even more dramatic by the flatness and the heat, that a lover tried to cross her courtyard and break a window. Then smiling as if she understood. Pulling on her little dress, her turquoise eyes gazing meditatively in the distance. Saying—(Lydia makes an effort to remember):

"The cop was kind of sympa-thetic."

Surely there was more.

"The god-dess will protect me."

Lydia feels the sweat increase around her neck. Somehow she'd imagined the dialogue between them more significant: Z.'s words floating theatrically across a summer night. Speaking of art and life. Her flat voice dominating the dilapidated café (for those who cared to listen). Or, at the Schubert Baths where they used to go to swim. With tiny black and white tiles, blue and white trim, open showers. Waiting for Z. to rub down with special creams from the health-food store (unguents, ointments, herbs distilled for use on hair, around the eyes, the heels). Lydia finally saying (leaning forward, granted, a little heftily): "Uh, I haven't seen you in ages." And Z. replying, head down (concentrating on the task), voice expressionless:

"Voyons donc, il faut cir-culer un peu."

In the hot air of the bar, Lydia suddenly feels like eating. Ice cream and steamy coffee. She hesitates, looking out the window. The sign-shop men are on the ladder. But no matter what the angle, the French-only version fails to cover the larger English-Hebrew-Arabic scripts showing underneath. In a lull in the music, the redhead (speaking French) mentions Ottawa again. Swinging her gaze, sea-coloured, even more limpid than before, under thick brows (formerly plucked so thin you could hardly see them), to look directly forward. The shoulders under her sleeveless top evoking summer travelling: a bus, the play of radios, the smell of gum. The bus station in Ottawa. The dusty road to the village near Ottawa, where Lydia's grandmother had a house.

Z. never spoke of origins. Her stiff but elegant stance covering (Lydia told herself) the lack of positive cultural images for a person growing up French in an English-dominant place. Like those girls dancing (prudently) by the Ottawa River in a bar near Lydia's grandmother's house. She knew them well, was always drawn to them. Frances (Françoise) Deguire standing round-shouldered on a village corner (in bright blue air and yellow daffodils). Saying, "We just broke up." Meaning she and Tracy, her effeminate Irish trucker lover. With panic in her voice. Although Frances (Françoise) was so tough she never cried: just kept everything inside her skinny boy's body. So when Lydia's grandmother said not to play with Frances (Françoise) any more, Frances (Françoise) only said: "Why?" And Lydia, trying to make the blow less personal, said: "Because I'm not allowed on the Back Street where you live." Seeing all the same how Frances (Françoise) could not shield the pain flickering over her green gaze, her face of an ash blonde.

Z. opted to mock the English by speaking their language perfectly. At the same time, using her Frenchness as a lure. Chin on hand, silk scarf tied perfectly around her neck in some Montréal café. Telling people the anecdotes they loved. Stories of excess. The cousin who died skydiving in a bikini, over Albany. The aunt in Ottawa who'd nearly caused a government to fall, due to a Parliamentarian lover's indiscretion. The voyeurs sitting round her—pale, thin arrivistes from English-speaking provinces—suspected her of tactics of diversion. Wanting to penetrate her mysteries. Couldn't she be more personal? Oddly, Lydia herself had never thought to come out and ask even the obvious thing directly: Why, in the new Québec where French came first, did Z. speak so frequently in English?

As if in … New Orleans.

In the third-floor window across the street, has not the pink flamingo changed its stance again? This time leaning sideways. Lydia, grown slightly bleary, due to focusing on a subject so … ephemeral. To regain equilibrium she orders cake with icing (like her mother used to make). Wondering why, in remembering, she only comes up with fragmented bits and pieces? Instead of anecdotes (the elements of a story). Images, obscuring key sensations—like the sparks that passed between them, even in their most banal conversations. Or, images, blotting certain details that would have helped her draw the portrait finely: how

Z. loved her mother, who (Z. claimed) had been a crashed pilot in another incarnation. (Lydia had seen this woman with her wild, sky-filled eyes.) Or, Z.'s generosity towards other women artists. Her sense of excellence. Going up to women at public conferences, praising their work with exactly the phrase that moved.

"Ton texte m'a fait trem-bler—"

Discreetly, politely, Lydia orders wine. Thinking how language is inadequate to synthesize Z.'s essence. If she tried again—in French? But—damn, the redhead's asking for the bill. She'll have to recall, faster, elements required to "round the picture out": Z. as temporary roommate (that hot day in the park when, with her hatbox, she asked to come and stay). Even then, Lydia gained no knowledge of her. Despite carefully watching Z.'s precise movements in the hot kitchen of her (Lydia's) apartment. Z. sitting in her (Lydia's) chair working at her typewriter. Lydia's cat sitting there beside her (equally enchanted). The phone was off the cradle. Maybe Z. was never intimate with anyone, at least in English (her only true friend, Lydia learned later, was a loyal Gemini as bilingual as she). Z. seeming to come close, but just when you wanted to get some reassurance regarding the security of the relationship, evading your control. She suddenly remembers that Z. wrote her twice to apologize after things got bad between them. She never really answered (hating confrontation).

Lydia's eyes close—to cover this mistake. Plus other truths about herself: her terrible romanticism. Preferring bits and pieces of the past, tattered flashes of Z., fragmented, with gaps both difficult to grasp and deliciously mysterious—to this serene, controlled figure sitting in the bar. Which figure has made of carefulness, of security, a science. Unless this excessive carefulness is only a layer over earlier ones: Z. sitting in the dilapidated café, hennaed hair brushed up in a cowlick. Or, the rich voice on the phone (elegant, yet teasing) saying: "Oh, oh my cat is eat-ing me." Or the almost titillating suspense of the ex-lover trying again to break her windows. What if something happened? Z. exhausted from getting up at night, checking for evidence of him in the darkened courtyard. Lydia intervening, she hoped non-offensively (it being near the end of the acquaintance, therefore her power substantially diminished). To say maybe loving women was more to the point. To which Z. replied (ironically?):

"Yeah, more and more are do-ing it."

Outside, the crumpled ball of paper is rolling down the sidewalk.

From her corner, Lydia sees the redhead standing up. Her clean, light form stretching lazily in the now vaguely dusky air of the noisy, smoky bar. Could that be a stretch of happiness? The loose pants have fallen perfectly around her tiny legs: not a stain or wrinkle. Lydia doesn't have to move any closer to sense the sweet odour of the skin. Redolent of those bath salts she never knew the name of. Z. was always *perfect* to a degree that was astounding, considering her poverty, her depressions. Now the redhead's on the street. Is that Z. pattering up the stairs? Maybe to get her suitcase? Or walking (her mother's daughter) towards the sky? Dressed lightly, simply, as if airy enough to fly.

Across the street the pink flamingo in the plant-box has turned around again. Now leaning back over the edge so far one of its wire legs is waving in the air. Lydia shifts (perspiring) in the hot yet air-conditioned bar. Wishing she still knew her. Nostalgic (despite herself) for their encounters in the dilapidated café. Where they sat in silence, almost, looking at the crumpled-up piece of paper outside the window, lodged against the wall. Z. suddenly getting up and running out. Lydia craning her neck to see the reason why: a taxi at the red light on the corner. Craning harder, Lydia could see a woman with short hair, small triangular face looking out the taxi's back window. Z. running after it. (Was there a snowbank?) Screaming as the taxi drove away:

"I love you, you bitch."

**(the sky is what I want)**

The bar as before. Outside it's dark. Making the stars—
rendered invisible from the ground by the bright, polluted
city—shine in their high arc over little gravel roofs with
giant saucer receptors on them, hemmed by tiny fake turrets, castellated parapets, painted tin cornices stretched
along their fronts.

Lydia's chair is empty.

..............................

..............................

Then she's back, impeccable as ever. From the
inner secret places to the tips of her fingers. A whiff of
her perfume floating by those regulars who happen to be
left (not the failed writer—gone, with his dirty, empty
briefcase—but the filmmaker, sagging at the knees,

drinking another beer in hopes of inspiration for his script; Ralph, swaying uncertainly in the middle of the room). Lydia sweeps by, surpassing them in endurance. With her little bag of tricks for staying relatively sober (used, discreetly, between portraits).

She smiles self-ironically. The "gag" is not funny—but her body (now she's stuck her finger down her gullet) is as cool as after-fever (just damp around the hairline); free of all that mushy-gushy liquid flowing around inside.

She steps towards her table. Precise, well-groomed hand pulling out her chair. Mind fixed purposefully on the peregrinations of the moment. Having definitely decided to spurn unwanted reminiscence (like that scene in the park, with the skinny girlish knee sticking out from underneath the blanket). Having also decided, behind the wooden door with the female cameo on it, to come down to earth a little. Head less in the clouds. So she doesn't turn into one of those silly women for whom the past is realer than the present (i.e., given undue emphasis). These thoughts all arising while kneeling in the cubicle staring at the turquoise stucco wall. Listening to two women outside at the makeup counter (beige Arborite with a spreading burn stain on it): both with long wavy permanents pinned back at the ears. One saying to the other:

"Sexual ... X ... [Lydia didn't grasp the word] is becoming so common. I mean people are really talking about it a lot ... But you can only get over it by working it out for yourself ... When it gets too much I get $100 worth of coke ... Well, what am I supposed to do? Jump off a bridge or something?"

Lydia sits gracefully. Her feet (in shoes with straps) planted firmly on the floor. Noting several chairs, oak-stained, only slightly more substantial than "kitchen," are empty. Nearly time to hit the road. Above them on the wall, a MOLSON sign half-blinking, so all you see is "MOI." The "MOI" reminding her of Z.'s ultimate withdrawal into a kind of egotism. I.e., a strong identifying narrative—including speaking only French—in order to gain confidence. Not that Lydia blames her. Because fragmented-type personae permit intruders, stepping in and operating secondary spaces of control. Full-time or occasionally. Like that fake-cheerful mother's voice being interviewed on the radio from her kitchen (likely green) in Verdun. After they found her daughter in the park. The mother saying she never knew how to reach her—but her daughter would call up, saying in her cute and peppy voice: "Hi, Mo-om. Everything's all right."

"Ev-ery-thing's all-right," mimes a meteorologist on the radio (slightly French accent). Speaking of the heat wave that's been going on for months. "*E-very-thing is normal, un-til proven o-therwise.*"

"Une Stella Artois," Lydia calls to the waitress: the new one passing by her table, touching, now, her shoulder and making her feel good. Lydia smiles, thinking: "I could grow old in this place." Where people are always touching and laughing it up like crazy. She means the Portuguese guys at the far end of the bar, gently sparring (physically and verbally). Or that older couple of Portuguese intellectuals, the woman a little stout with wire-rimmed glasses, sitting at a table reading European newspapers, comfortable and happy. Lydia imagines them in some café in Lisbon. Maybe the café on the cliff by the gateway to the Alfama. Looking down on the bay, which shines absolute gold at dusk. Later: full of twinkling lights of ships as if the water were the sky.

"Plus a brandy chaser," she adds, partly to be nice. Partly because she hasn't entirely sobered up and doesn't want to either. Not that she minds returning to her empty room. (Fake fireplace. No phone. Formica-covered kitchen.) More real at a distance, as at the end of a telescope.

After this, she'll go—

She gazes, content, at her domain. Taking in the throbbing dance music, under which (unfortunately) an anxious voice is rising:

"... so *depressed,* I couldn't stand the air. Had to step out to take a breath. Then you ask someone for help and they say: 'Oh, no, sir, I have to go to the bank. Come back later.' And you come back and they're gone. It's fine to drive around in a new car and look elegant. But you have to think of others. If you make them feel bad, they end up so depressed ..."

"He needs to take some distance—," she thinks, glancing out the window. Knowing that under the invisible stars' high, dizzying arc, the long ever-narrowing street's still climbing towards where the sun set earlier. Lined with closed storefronts. Dark glass, signalling the importance of obliqueness: i.e., a *thing* can reflect a multitude of others. Like a gesture in a photo, pointing outside the frame. Or History, if told through constellations of signs or images (as well as laws and principles). Example:

History told through smell (since smell's the Queen of senses). She thinks of her "brides" on the roof. If kissed on the nape, the telling odours they'd emit. Nanette, slightly lemon; Adèle of Halifax, violet; the woman who went to Cuba, sandalwood; Z., herbal, yet rigorously exotic; Ivory for the dyke from the West. Some of them are dancing behind the fake Turkish domes, swag-trimmed cornices with pointy spears, or finials, on the corners, jabbing at the sky. And down below, the bar, slightly in a lull while people wolf down odours of grilled chicken, fries, rice, beer, smoke, old mussels in vinegary peppery sauce, fish and sauerkraut.

Her own scent is musk.

She takes out her mirror. To see how "musk" translates into image: something slightly animal. Thinking (the mirror's slightly foggy), one of these days, she'll do a portrait of the woman she sees there: Herself—some time back (the past not dangerous or nostalgic if telescoped by the present). Maybe something kind of Cubist, organized in fragments held together by her present knowledge of the subject. Say, at the point she moved farther east in order to change her ways. Fasting, translating (just a little). Walking. Cutting every contact, except the magic of the Inuit. Himself totally cut off—

"The guilt of self-assertion," says a woman two tables over, puffing on a cigarette, "is like the guilt of doing art."

The music throbs harder.

Lydia lights up too (although her stomach's queasy), thinking, "on the contrary, a woman can create herself from nothing." Example: fasting as an antidote to drinking (which fasting she'll start again tomorrow). Growing slimmer (then blowing up, then growing slim again). Until as sleek as Z. Lydia puts away her mirror, feeling for a minute, that the best part in Z.'s portrait was looking out and seeing the men across the street with their ladder. Walking up and down. Then putting up the sign. Which projection outward gave Lydia (she didn't know why) a huge rush of relief.

She slowly sips her brandy.

"He thinks I'm beautiful," says a voice (soft Latin accent).

"What a stroke of luck!" (voice of friend, possibly ironic).

"But it's so hard living up to that. All my energy's gone. I just want to crash out exhausted. Is this reality or what?"

Lydia sips some more. Wondering if "reality" comprises what's just gone by in the mind, or what's in the process of unfolding. Wondering how much of this might be comprised in History. Outside on the sidewalk—some kind of dealer, and his clients. "*African,*" says someone. "Your narrative's racist," says another. Plus various other discourses morcelled in the air: the meaning of perversion ("an apricot-flavoured prick," a voice suggests hopefully); or of "Canadian" (answer unclear), safe sex, serial killers. The parade of fashion going by the window, ever more chaotic, signifying the end of an era. Farther along in the dark, two women coming towards each other like dancers: same sensuality; love. Desperation. The two guys who were just on the sidewalk sitting down behind her. One, round and confident, saying to his friend (thin, dread-knots, features so tense his face lines are blue):

"Il s'est fait déporter."

"Mais c'est pas juste à cause de toi, c'est certain."

She sits very still (the clock says 11:25). Registering how (also feeling nauseous) a few halogen spots brighten the tops of patrons' heads. A song called *Co-caine* starting on the radio (some late-night station). Reminding her, for some reason, that her problem with reality is that she (like her grandfather) is a philosopher of sorts. Always wanting (seeing) something more. As when he used to look at pictures of her boyfriends and tell her, based on something in their faces, many things about them.

"C'était donc un Indien?" a Québécoise asked her once.

"Non, *méditerranéen.*"

And that's all about her background that she intends to reveal.

The radio plays louder (her feet tapping on the floor).

"She's slowly going crazy from being alone all the time," says a voice, very close.

Lydia sips her beer (intense mockery in her eye). Which eye meets (accidentally) the dark, almost angry gaze of the famous poet from San Francisco (the one in the suit leaning on the bar between the Portuguese and the regulars). Who earlier was watching her more positively. Now on his way out the door, his hunched shoulders edging across the street. But, Lydia (having trouble focusing) returns to her portrait: anecdotal fragments organized—but not too rigorously—with a little space around them to open possibilities. Like Aztec art in the sense that their figures, carved on parapets, seemed projected towards the endless blue. Of course, under this dreamlike surface, lay darker, more insidious narratives promising ultimate disaster. Requiring more and more sacrifices in hopes of reprieve—

The bar door bangs open. And a woman, basically attractive, but red blotches on her face, top hanging off a shoulder, races wildly in. A syringe full of blood held before her like a weapon. People falling back from her · path as quickly as they can. In case she has AIDS. As she rushes around the room (looking for someone). Then, outside again, racing by the window. Past a van painted blue with white clouds on it. Plus, in red, the words (barely visible in the dim light of the streetlamp): I'M ONE OF THE HAPPIER GUYS IN THE WORLD.

Lydia gets up, feeling strange (for a minute). Again almost dancing around her table. Then sits down, eyes fixed on the sign across the street: LA CHARCUTERIE HEBRAÏQUE (bright white and orange). Right beside it: DÉGUSTER LE MEILLEUR POULET AU QUÉBEC: SANDWICH À LA CASTANHEIRA. Rustling her legs slightly to feel the stretch of fragrant "silk" between them. Thinking that (for her portrait), the materiality of the body in its particular expression might be a sign of this point of the century. Example: what she had for breakfast. Or the things hanging in her closet. Her brand of cigarettes. What she did for sex? True, it went missing from the facts—once she threw the Inuit out. After which he watched her tracks in the snow. "At about ten a.m. you went out; at three came back," he'd say, pointing. The displaced curve of his body (the curve of the trapper), tragic. With its memory of the grace of animals and people singing in nights of stoned eternity. Him moving like a bird on the tundra. The little ducks he tried to carve flying with greater and greater difficulty through the concrete holes of the city.

But—nearly time to go.

She lights a cigarette. Perspiration running down her torso under the material of her blouse. Not as crisp as earlier. Absorbing (by osmosis) the bar vibrating with the dull thuds of tanked people starting to drift out. Having stuffed themselves with grease. And drunk enough to feel loose. So they can go to Balatou, or La Playa, or even one of the North American French-style clubs along the street. Pretending to dance authentically.

Her feet, shod like the Portuguese woman's, with precise little heels, tap (impatiently) to the music. While she tries to think how she was at a point in the past. Remotely aware of the late-nighters starting to drift in. A mix of boring drunks without any stamina left—yet capable of violence (one—his arm around the waitress, the one Lydia likes, with a single braid down her back, clinging top and skirt—pretending to be friendly, his nails in her flesh). Plus their opposites, the night-walkers: loners, trying to stay anonymous.

Like herself, Lydia, since that boxed-in winter—

## Donkey Riding

*1.* The weather forecast said dull, grey and rainy. And it wasn't kidding, Lydia thought, entering the bar. Wearing jeans and a plaid shirt, topped by a short, now damp black jacket for flair (at the time, still only giving in a little to the 80s-business-look). But no sooner was she seated in her favourite darkish corner, ready to relax, with the smell of espresso coffee bubbling in the machine, raunchy music, French and Portuguese voices. Nothing English to interrupt her train of thought. When she noticed some interference in her line of vision. A woman in a red coat saying loudly, intrudingly, in English, to the waitress that she'd come from Toronto. Because she could sense a real effervescence in this place. Just like Paris in the 20s. The woman ran her fingers through her hair, bleached and a wave over the brow for added interest. "Also, the rents are cheap."

"Yeah, Paris," thought Lydia. "Paris Troika." (She'd always thought perestroika was a dance until she read in the newspaper it meant: capitalism.) But even as she eyed the woman from Toronto, her stomach felt like a small animal's in the forest when it senses trouble (change) arriving. Soon they'd be here in masses. Renting the cheap apartments with their business acumen. Filling the space a person needed to reflect with their hegemonizing standards. Discussed in loud, overconfident voices. Meanwhile appropriating every new idea. Watching across the bar, she saw that woman's ambitious red lips tremble (pretending to be shy) as she tried to strike up a conversation with the guys at the next table. Sarcastically, Lydia hummed a tune:

*Were you e-ver in Qué-bec*
*Donkey riding, donkey riding.*

"What do you do, are you artists?" the woman said.

"Unemployment insurance."

"Oh," smiling, "uh, how do you say that in French?"

"Travailleur autonome," said one of the guys. The other killed himself laughing.

2. Thank god, next time that woman wasn't there. Lydia settled back into her grey, immensely satisfying afternoons. Walking down the half-block by the park. She infinitely preferred grey to all others. It flattened reminiscence. Turning left at the Grey Nuns' fence. Right to her favourite bar-café. With Ralph the drunken sailor, a guy in ponytail staring at the video screen, the stripper coming in for her "afternoon primer": cherry red, very alcoholic. Lydia's kind of people. Also the place was like a cabin, tongue 'n' groove walls. So homey she could easily sink into a state of concentration. To indulge in her obsession of the period: the daily writing down of dreams ... *Then*

*I'm riding on a horse, so large it could be Trojan. With another rider (possibly a woman) and a baby boy, very sweet, but who will likely turn out criminal. The horse crosses green fields in the direction of my disapproving parents.*

So into it she didn't even notice right away that the woman in the red coat had returned. Sitting crossing, uncrossing her legs, trying to attract attention. Lydia had to laugh at how two truck drivers with quarts of beer between them at the next table ignored the bitch completely. "That damn truck. I rammed her up good at, at … I can't remember the name, ya know, the weekend in October when they take the turkey out and put it on the table," said one. The other, a francophone, looked perplexed. "Ya know, the turkey," said the first guy leaning down as if picking up something heavy and putting it on the table. "C'est quoi ça?" said the French guy, calling to the waitress. The guy speaking English again went through his routine of picking up the turkey and putting it on the table. But the waitress, who spoke both the official (French) and unofficial (English) language without an accent, not to mention Portuguese, didn't know what it's called either, that weekend when they get out the big turkey and put it on the table (neither the French nor Portuguese have it). Lydia's face was collapsing in an expression of hilarity, so she couldn't have stood up and shouted "Thanksgiving!" if she'd wanted to.

"Hé toé," said the Québécois to the woman in the red coat. "De quoi y parle?" pointing to his friend.

"Sorry," said the woman. "I can't understand a word you're saying, I only speak international French."

Lydia was just waiting for the woman to say something like that. She squeezed her fists in pleasure, trying to think of the second verse of that old *Donkey* song sailors used to sing while loading the riches of Québec on the decks of British ships. Something about the king with golden crown coming to take the lumber.

*3.* Fortunately, again the woman disappeared. And Lydia settling daily deeper in. Preferably with her back against the wall (not to look at some small stuffed animal from Portugal they'd put up recently). Her head either in profile to the window or looking out directly. The bar not crowded. Outside the window: a grey December sky with some early snowflakes in it (she's Sagittarius rising). Sitting there, content with her choices. The move farther east to get away from people. Writing another dream. Also about a horse ... *It must have been a male, because I was very attracted to it. A wild little horse, standing outside the window. The attraction so strong, he crashed right through the glass. I left through the front door with C., a lesbian I know ...* When she heard that woman's voice again. Pitched a little nasally. But with less clipped, less tight-assed pronunciation. As if already softened by the colour of her surroundings: the kind of wilful laxness freely cultivated in those cities of the Americas where English doesn't dominate.

"She's crazy about her litterbox."

Lydia sat, suspended (gleefully anticipating).

"She always has her nose in it, sniffing, sniffing. I have to clean it constantly." The woman's full painted lips

parted slightly in a knowing smile. Half-guilty, half-aston-
ished as if vaguely sexually excited. With that expression
and her red coat open at the shoulders, revealing, under
a tight sweater, a pair of magnificent large breasts—
the resemblance to Marilyn Monroe was unmistakable.
Marilyn, tailored Toronto version.

"What's your name?" interrupted the pock-marked
guy beside her, getting interested. The blonde hesitated.
Her hand against her cheek. Then continuing (Lydia'd
already noticed she had a very determined chin) to say
exactly what she wanted: "A real perfectionist. Once I forgot to clean it and she wouldn't go near it. I can't leave her
out too long, in case she has to go. She comes *inside* for
that—"

"What's your name?" said the pock-marked guy
again. Lydia'd seen him here before. Bragging to a mousy
little woman (the kind that likes to make men feel comfortable regarding the functions of their bodies) that his
main ambition—apart from directing a film with himself
in it—was a good shit every morning.

"What's your name, eh?"

"Norma jean."

An almost sly smile played on Lydia's pale lips (no
lipstick yet, given her carried-over 70s image). She should
have known this woman was a fake. She could almost be a
drag queen. No, that wouldn't be fair to queens. Lydia
picked up her pen, pausing only another minute to wonder what that woman was doing in this town. Maybe getting set up in business (some kind of art agent or
communicator). Forgetting, naturally, she didn't know the

language. Like some of those spoiled little Wasps, the students, starting to come in here. Ruining the ambience. Teeth too white, hand-sewn leather knapsacks, sturdy shoes. Straight from the suburbs.

But the vision of Norma jean's mother that rose up in Lydia's mind was different: poor but shrewd. Maybe a waitress at Murray's on Bloor Street. Therefore wanting more for her daughter. She may even have given her daughter that expensive red coat to conceal her full figure. "Never play up your resemblance to Marilyn Monroe," her mother told her once. "In dress, conservative equals classy. I should have known why your father insisted on giving you that name."

Or, maybe Lydia was projecting her own mother's attitude in similar situations. She thought of Norma jean in some white room she'd rented (combination studio and flat). Dirt cheap, so thinking she'd made a coup. Sitting on a bed, winding a strand of smooth, well-cut blonde hair around her finger. Noticing that the walls bulge, making corner joints wavy instead of straight. Due to inadequate sewers, draining at the level of the street. Causing activity in the foundations. To the point of buildings sometimes leaning over. In the mirror, an old three-foot cast-iron radiator with flower patterns on it.

A white Persian kitten stretched out on top.


4. Saturday, somewhere near the start of winter: the light is grey. Lydia entered the bar, her skin prickling happily with the sudden rush of warmth, the odour of cigarette smoke and coffee. Under the arm of her second-hand

man's camel-hair coat, the arts section of *Le Devoir*. So hoping beautiful D., whose red hair flashes like an emblem winter and summer from her bicycle along The Main, wouldn't drop in for a chat after her swim at the Schubert Baths. Lydia pulled out her chair (back to the corner). And looked around (as was her habit). Oh god—that woman Norma jean. Who'd put on glasses, and was looking good-natured and relaxed. With the pock-marked guy again. Basking, almost, in his (too-) generous physical presence: that healthy animal smell he has due to a good shit every day. Albeit, probably sometimes his maleness smells too rich, making Norma jean slightly nauseous. She'd get over it by focusing on how she loves a man who understands, respects the functions of the body. Never rushing her. Gently touching—

The guy's hand rose. "In imposing French signs, they're taking away our human rights," he said loudly. Indicating the sign across the street, in English, Hebrew, Arabic, that would soon be covered with French only. Waving at it dramatically, as if this were a play. Norma jean's cool paw stiffened in his warm one. Ultimately withdrawing. Still, Lydia hummed (preventatively) a line from *Donkey Riding*.

> *Were you ever in Québec,*
> *Stowing timber on a deck*
> *Donkey riding, donkey riding ...*

Imagining Norma jean (improving maybe, but still too dependent on codes from elsewhere to understand this place). Sitting on the bed in the white room she'd rented. Across the room, her computer, waiting for her to get her day started. Writing up CVs. But first she'd steal a minute from her perfectly planned routine: exercise, high-fibre breakfast—

Lydia looked out. The sidewalk was full of people rushing by. With bags of vegetables from Warshaw's, bran bread from the bakery, fish from Waldman's. No, Waldman's was on strike. The workers, mostly Portuguese, outside its broken windows waving placards (like weak arms in a losing battle) with their cold-water-reddened hands. The passing sacks of groceries, weighted down with meat, making Lydia recall a dream in which *she's asking somebody to look after her horse while she works. It's quite a wild little horse.* She took her pen to write. The dream in turn recalling the eroticism of an erected horse she saw as a child. Standing in a field beyond a window at her grand-mother's. The erection beautiful, dark red. Then, as now, the image disturbed vaguely. Lydia bent her head and wrote: *After, my horse and I are in a field. A lot of tenderness. I feel guilty (there is a house from which somebody might be watching), and nauseated. But I felt I could do it if I could be on top.*

Her pen slipped to the floor. Bending over to recover it, she glanced surreptitiously up. That Norma jean was watching, her pert little chin, red made-up lips, outlined by the light from the window.

5. For a while, Lydia didn't see Norma jean. Not that she even noticed. She had other things to think about. Keeping control of her existence so it wouldn't bleed into the surrounding chaos. Waking, working on translation,

breakfast. The rest of the day given over to wandering. Eyes straight ahead. Strong and solitary. Her neighbours, French, sensing her trace of accent, leaving her completely to herself. Yes, this was the life for her. The space to focus on her dreams. Dreams were getting to be the best part of the day. She loved holding them in her mind for hours before she wrote them down. Usually late afternoon.

On this anticipatory note Lydia wandered towards the bar. Mid-December, and the sky as grey as only a sky can be. Watching a sitcom in successive windows. Then displays of books. Clothes (a sweater with sequined leopard roaring from the bust). Marilyn in a beauty-salon glass, soft large breasts delicately contained in shell-coloured silk halter-top. "She's everywhere these days," thought Lydia, entering the bar. Looking forward to the coffee, the relaxing mix of voices. But Ralph was banging too loudly on the table. Also, that Norma jean again. Head leaning intimately towards the pock-marked guy's (named Rod). Lydia lowered her eyes in mock embarrassment at the unattractiveness of the object. Just as Norma jean stood up, coat buttoned from top to bottom. Saying something haughty. And slamming out the door.

Lydia picked up her pen. And wrote the title of her dream: *What Lack of Territory Brings a Woman To.* Imagining, for a minute, Norma jean padding across the white rug in her flat to get dressed for power. The better not to repeat the misfortunes of her mother. Who, in order to cheer up when she came home from Murray's, putting her beautiful shapely legs, more and more deformed with purple veins, on the teak coffee-table, would ask Norma jean to make her popcorn. The daughter knew the percentage in gracefully acceding. Standing very straight under a white sweater and blue wool pants that pricked a little, shaking the pan over the hot gas stove, she imagined with resentment her mother at the restaurant. Pretending to warm up, to be the understanding woman for some dry-beaked guy gazing from his bleary, helpless eyes, and saying: "Tell me dear, what in god's name should I have for breakfast?" Her mother could be polite to the worst people to get her tips, thought Norma jean, who wanted to be an artist. Knowing the answer in advance:

"Oh god, Norma jean, no

"A woman needs money

"To control existence."

After which, Norma jean moved out. First, to a white room in Toronto. (Lydia was in that city once: she remembers streets with people on them, yet strangely empty. Like in Montréal during the October Crisis.) The room not far from her mother's flat in the back of a huge old house owned by Mr. Moura from Portugal. Where they'd moved from the suburbs after the father skulked out. Rugs, pretty curtains. Her mother's feet on the coffee-table, waiting, sad but confident. Having given her daughter everything after the father left, especially Discipline. These were Norma jean's thoughts, standing nearby on the ugly corner of College and Ossington. A squat grey Royal Bank on one side. A dirty red-brick Y on the other. Waiting for the streetcar. In the red coat, a neat fake-alligator case in her hand. Her reflection in the bank window, distorted, due to the forbidding sobriety of the light. "I have to get out of this place," she said to herself.

Lydia could see her, now, in the room she'd rented (dirt cheap) in Montréal. Pulling on a black sweater, black skirt over the perfect figure. Ideally what she wanted was to be a publicist for some Québécois modern dance group. They're among the best in the world. The other day she saw one of the blonde dancers, hurrying along the street. In long navy tightly tailored coat and fuchsia-coloured gloves. So that against the white snow and sky she appeared to be on stage. Norma jean sighed, pulling on her own red A-line coat, putting keys and makeup and very clean brush into her medium-square purse. Wondering as she did how the French got to be so efficient, given the time they spend at lunch. Opening the door, she stepped into the crooked stair-lined street. Experiencing a moment of nostalgia for the soft fur of her beautiful white cat. Who didn't come back after she put it out one morning.

On the sidewalk, her purse popped open.

It wasn't the first time that damn purse popped open.

6. Still December: the snow falling in small drops with infinitely large spaces. As in a premature thaw. Lydia came in, hoping, as usual, for no one to interrupt her train of thought. She wanted to sit and think. The bar was fairly dark, like everywhere at this time of year. She undid her scarf, sitting very far back, under two paintings in gold frames of a sheepish lion and a roaring jaguar by F. Lopès

on the tongue 'n' groove wall. Closing her eyes, she took in the ambience: different languages, dishes, the video machine (silent for a minute). A busty blonde cartoon lying on its screen, legs up, waiting for a shot of loonies to start it buzzing, flashing.

The bar door opened, admitting—possibly Norma jean (Lydia couldn't tell from there). The woman walking quickly and calling in her overconfident (yet somehow tremulous) voice: "Appohr-tay-moi une be-ère." (Lydia mocked the accent.) The woman's lipstick heavy, making her skin look greyer than Lydia remembered. Also (maybe it was the light), the woman seemed to display a greater virility of bone structure than N.j.'s spoiled little mug. At least the woman's partner was an improvement: layered blond hair, wide sailor-style pants and shoes. Likely some French-speaking artist.

"So she got what she wanted," Lydia thought ironically.

Wishing she could warn that guy how those types from Toronto have a reputation for coming to the cultures of the margins. And ripping off ideas. This happened once to Lydia—at a feminist demonstration! One of those instances where you meet somebody whose face you like and they like yours, and the two of you start talking, talking. Extending it later to Le Caffe Internationale, under the underpass since 1935, to eat spumoni gelato and drink cappuccino. Lydia confiding she was an obsessive storyteller (like her grandfather used to be). Except she could never finish things. So one day (kind of joking), she would "likely" write a book of portraits called

*Installation with Muddy Frames.* Then, what to her surprise, but a few months later that bitch had opened a show back in T.O. with precisely the same name. Who, when confronted with the injustice (she had the nerve to call when she visited Montréal), blinked her innocent eyes of a blonde and said:

"I never denied I was influenced by you."

Remembering this, Lydia's heart beat madly.

She tried to focus on writing down the dream she'd had last night. Glancing just once again towards the window where "Norma jean" looked even more like M.M. than usual, given how she'd glamorized her makeup. Also, wearing unusually funky clothes: kneelength pants, striped stockings, large shoes. Later, walking by Lydia's table to the can, it was clear she had hardly any breasts. So someone else completely. It occurred to Lydia that M.M. was a trope for something currently in the air. She didn't know what.

She wrote down her title. *A House Dream, Rather Than a Horse Dream* (all her dreams had titles). Wondering where the real Norma jean was. Maybe still fixing up her lair with cool efficiency for some coup. Her computer set up under the best window (its frame painted black in contrast with the white white walls). The Persian cat still absent. The place possibly a little too cosy for efficiency. Oh, but she usually ultimately got what she wanted. Although, she couldn't help noticing that people here reacted to her differently. As if the change of place had made her lose her confidence. Unlike Toronto where she knew what people wanted. Where men lit up to her (useful from the point of view of business). In love, however, only wanting them until they wanted her. Her popularity—something she never shared with her mother, despite their little chats over popcorn in the evenings. This was odd because her mother would have been reassured to have her sleep with other men.

Other than who?

Lydia stared uncomfortably at a bear walking over a beer ad on the wall. That last phrase had popped up incongruously. While, in the back of Lydia's mind, in a sudden decisive gesture, Norma jean stood up by her bed, ripped off her slip and pulled on her jeans. Which fit nicely over her tight little hips. Then moved hopefully to the window. Looking down into the bright, tin-shed lined alley for the cat. The little fake. After all that fuss about its litterbox, pretending it couldn't go without it, staying away all night. She could wring its neck.

Animals bring out the best and worst in people.

Lydia wrote: *In a country cottage with my father. Outside a large hairy bear. I am very scared. I try to lock the door. But it has a very thin screen the bear can easily tear. My father acts as if it doesn't matter* ... While (still in the corner of her mind) Norma jean was standing, back to the room, her white nape exquisite under the blonde bob, thinking how she'd love to m-mush her face in the cat's long hair.

7. Sunday in the heart of winter. Lydia, up since dawn. The world all crackling white and empty. On her walk to the bar, every curtain drawn. Carefully, she pulled out her chair in the completely silent room. Noticing as she sat,

behind her on the wall, not the gold-framed painting of a spotted jaguar or flaming lion signed F. Lopès. But the head of a laughing mother fox. Under which they'd mounted, on the same board, a tiny baby fox's head. This made her feel like crying.

But Lydia was against doubling back on narrative. Instead she focused on all the empty chairs. The profile of an empty chair: always so full of promise. Her favourite paintings and photographs were of empty chairs on deserted café terraces in Berlin or Paris—. Feeling better, she sniffed the espresso the waitress put before her. Rubbing her hands (the place still cold, due to lack of clients). As the door opened and a young couple entered. His pained words "shafted" and "insincerity" crossing the pale, used-up air (still full of last night's cigarette smoke). Her pained voice, believing his good intentions. "But we're at a stalemate." He turning abruptly on his heel, angry at her "failure to see what I mean." She (soft brown hair), sad but determined, took up her pen and wrote.

Lydia smoothed her placemat in order to do the same. Her dream, still a little buried by waking up this morning thinking of all those sad people who stayed home last night, therefore, early birds on Sunday. With nothing on TV but the racket of evangelists. Also, an empty bar is never at its best in natural light. Spotted tablecloths. Swept dirty floors. A crack across the mirror. She wondered what Norma jean was up to. Hadn't seen her in ages. Maybe taking advantage of one of these endless Sunday mornings to redo her CV (Lydia should do the same). But first sitting still a minute, examining the objects in the room: black plastic stand on her desk to hold her papers while she worked. White rug, white quilt on the low futon with black pillows on it. Leaning back, strap off one alabaster shoulder, to watch the evangelist on TV in a tight suit shake his fist and sweat. Her mother found such postures "provocative." Unconsciously, N.j. straightened. Albeit, thinking if she could get a French guy she'd remedy him of a few biases regarding the stodginess of the English.

For a moment, Lydia (unable to remember a single word from the dream she'd had last night) felt almost drawn to her. With her exaggerated drag-queen way of leaning her shoulders forward. Seductive, but hard as nails under the fake-deferential exterior. The ability to steel herself no doubt useful when trying to start a business. So that if the client laid out his reasons for not wanting her as agent or publicist, she'd be listening carefully, betraying not one iota of her hurt feelings. This way of letting acumen seep into the depths of art and relationships, learned from her mother. Who used to tell her: "Do as I say to avoid the past impinging."

Or else it was some more of that father stuff coming out?

This last thought stopped Lydia in her tracks.

Again the bar door opened. Blowing in a waft of cold air, and an older couple with it. Endimanché, the way older people are, coming in from mass. Perfect press of pants, polish of the shoes, shine of the glasses. As if neatness could make up for their lack of former dash. The man's scarred, lined face speaking very fast in French:

"Alors, mon frère est mort. So *bye-bye*. Je m'occupe des vivants, moi."

Lydia drifted, both attracted and repulsed, back to the white room (snowing again outside, though less and less, because of the greenhouse effect). Rod (the pockmarked one) having just left, angry because she hadn't been able to sleep with him: the smell. Leaning back, the pink négligé strap again hanging off her white shoulder, she wished to hug her cat. Why couldn't humans smell like that? She was having more and more trouble using her charms to get what she wanted. What if she needed to borrow money? She'd become so inefficient lately. *What's wrong with this town?*

*Were you e-ver in Québec,* hummed Lydia.
*Where you'd break your bleedin' neck*
*Riding on a donkey.*

Comparing, in her mind, Toronto, the industrial centre of English Canada, very Protestant in its way of thinking. And this place's equally business-oriented, but different, codes of accessibility. Here, too, every group of people trying to outdo the other (although a deeper layer of chronic unemployment). Telephones on restaurant tables jangling endlessly during longer business lunches. However, on the street, indications of a barely controlled propensity towards excess: la barmaid d'une after-hours, now entering, bracelets from elbow to wrist. Tight velvet pants, silk polka-dot top open on little camisole, sunglasses, makeup. Those rooftops with their crumbling or renovated cornices decked with bows, draping, stars, flowers. Stairs leading from one gable down to another.

And from there to still a lower level on which was written in large, uneven letters: BAZAR.

"Bizarre," sighed Norma jean. Examining the plaster cherubs dancing round the fixtures. There was something about this place she hadn't understood. Something—possibly her mother had given her a clue: she tried to concentrate. Her head more full of warnings from childhood (her mother gave so many) than memories. Such as the older woman's restraining look in the workroom in the suburban bungalow where they lived before her father left. With its spring shaft of light and the smell of new-cut wood. The daughter and her father turning lathes, with her mother Sherry's shadow watching from the corner of the door. But when her mother went up to check something on the stove, her father put his hand on the stomach of Norma jean's sweater. Which had a slippery effect because of the nylon camisole underneath.

In the bar Lydia crossed out *The Persian Cat Is Absent.* Then she wrote: *A wide-open window. From which a white cat is flying. Feet splayed, fine white hair streaming against the grey sky. Me, Lydia, watching with my brother. He, looking down, sees a horse standing in a field. Do horses lay eggs? he asks. I know better than to answer. Do horses lay eggs? he asks again. Despite myself, I look down. If they did— It Would Protect My Mother.*

Underlining *It Would Protect My Mother.* Feeling slightly weird.

8. February 10: The sun's rays through thick clouds giving everything a particularly dramatic backdrop. The bar door

opened and Lydia swaggered in. Second-hand man's coat unbuttoned at the throat. Trying to look arrogant. Having walked very fast plop plop through the slush. Away from the osteopath's. From the osteopath's dark-stained doors, her dim stucco hall, her brown-toned interior. From the osteopath's thick black curls, white skin, bright red lips. Hands, kneading Lydia's body. Kneading kneading the knotted back—until something budged inside. Some huge solid mass like a giant turd trying to come out the top of her head. "Cry, Lydia, cry," the osteopath said, her cheek against Lydia's. But the thing got stuck halfway. Lydia got up. Padding with her skinny legs and slightly pointed feet across the floor (awkward in an old T-shirt and yesterday's underwear).

Lydia pulled out her chair. In a corner, Norma jean, naturally. But Lydia couldn't bother—. She stared out the dirty window, fighting off a wave of disgust. At how the dramatic sky turned the foreground into ugliness. Including the half of Norma jean's face reflected in the spotty pane: peony lips, carefully pencilled eyebrows, freckled with the dirt. Wearing (under the red coat) some taffeta thing from the 50s. Definitely an improvement. Maybe she was learning. Still, Lydia tried (half-enthusiastically) to remember the phrase from *Donkey Riding* about how *the gals in Québec put on a show, a-wagglin' and dancin'*. Ralph-the-sailor's medals clanging metallic as he rose impatiently to his feet. Making her headache worse.

She wondered if Norma jean ever felt like this? Waking with a start in the white room at six a.m. (still no cat), did she often sit a minute on the edge of her bed to let the same sudden heaviness in her pass? What was it? She'd never felt so black, so weighted down, before. Also, the curtains hung suspiciously still in the open window. She got up and ran to look below. Feeling as guilty as if she'd lost a child. Yet also relief: no dirty litterboxes, cat hairs stuck to everything, cat whining. She didn't mean that: she missed its heart-shaped face looking up insistingly, demandingly. The softness that she wanted to devour. She looked harder: small footprints leading under the courtyard fence. Oh no, maybe the poor thing waited, then froze to death somewhere.

But Norma jean knew how to counter negativity of feeling by jumping to her feet. Pulling on her clothes. Jeans. Those big boots it's so hard to get into. She had to find it: if not, she killed it by killing its self-esteem. By loving loving loving, then suddenly rejecting it: getting up at night when it was rolling, rolling that plastic thing along the hall, *clink, cling, clang, clank.* Wanting to throw it against the wall. Also, that cat would never get under the covers with her. Sometimes she'd try to force it. Wishing soft furry animals were more full-length to hug. Then the cat would retreat, nose in the air, as if offended by her smell.

Lydia imagined Norma jean opening the wooden gate ... walking through the alley (in the bar, her eyes sneaking a glance at her). Ohhhh—nice and fresh, the new snow shining like diamonds to raise her spirits. Stepping carefully through the whiteness, the woollen arm of her coat moving tight under her nose to block the stench of cat piss from a broken-down garage door.

Obviously a cat hideout. She gave it a kick, never knowing if that cat was really deaf or just ignored people. Otherwise—sheer perfection. Sensual, clean, courageous, its perfect body language: every motion entirely symmetrical. Due to the fact that the vast majority of kittens, like certain privileged people, have ideal childhoods. It made her so angry the way Tink and her sister Blue would lie there on the floor purring purring, until they fell back, swooning with the aftertaste of mother in their little noses.

She wanted to tear them right away from the tits.

Lydia's wry smile turned back into the feeling of disgust. She stared at the spots on the window, now fading in the dusk. She knew that woman (today, just quietly staring out) was weird; she knew it from the first. Maybe it had to do with background: spoiled rotten. So, as a child, tons of self-assurance. Pink and white and active. Her father even called her Jim, for she was his companion. The little girl, at first almost in love. But growing bolder, more condescending as she ripened. It happens that a child's angle of perception suddenly gets diverted. At the table with her mother, suddenly turning and calling him a weakling. A failure as a man. He took it speechlessly. Outside the yellow kitchen window were three elms Norma jean had drawn before they got cut down. Plus a driveway leading to a street. Minus sidewalks to discourage people walking.

The street led to a shopping plaza.

Some mimosas.

9. Before she knew it. *March.* Coming to the bar, Lydia saw vague swellings on the branches. Shivering, she sat. Hating this time of year. *Too* much grey on grey. At night the alleys were dark and muddy. To walk in them was just inviting trouble. She wrote down a title: *Trouble in the House.* Noticing Norma jean, or else her skinnier double (Lydia couldn't tell) several tables over. If Norma jean, definitely getting funky. Maybe gazing in the mirror (the white room stretching out behind her), she told herself: "I'm going to put darker shadow on my lids, I want to look worldly. I'm going to let my hair go wild—. A slap in the face of all those pa-pa-ternalizing men who—." Lydia checked herself from getting too ridiculous. Anyway, it wasn't the real N.j. because the guy in sailor pants was with her. Whose blue serge arm N.j.'s double now touched in a very feminine gesture. Saying in a loud, quite masculine contralto: "I like their fragile look after fucking—"

Lydia stared at a sign above the bar. Buttoning her plaid shirt neatly from the top to the bottom. Feeling out of kilter. The sign said: FOR SPRING, FRESH FROM NEW YORK: GÂTEAU AU FROMAGE. Recalling the day she saw *that* "Norma jean's" face in a hairdresser's window. Not the one on The Main with the real M.M.'s picture in it. But on one of those little horizontal streets that jab into the mountain. The face, wistful in its makeup, and wild blonde hair (actually made of plastic) flying out behind. Feeling curious, she'd gone in for a haircut. A strident song about eating black lobster played on the tape deck. Watching the enthusiastic way this "Norma jean's" torso (in loose shorts over black-striped tights) lunged forward, hips out behind, to tackle someone's hair, Lydia had wondered: "Do I say she or he?" Someone called him Jess. Beside Jess, the pseudo-sailor's smooth forehead creased in concentration as he applied purple colour to a dykey woman's hair. Lydia listened carefully to their conversation, hearing nothing but a recipe for broccoli and tofu.

Picking up her coffee (plaid shirt still buttoned), Lydia switched to the table right behind them. Sitting with her back in their direction to hear their conversation. Noticing, as she sat, the greyness of the five-o'clock shadow under "N.j.'s" powder. Also the long hooped skirt, Quaker-style shoes with thick soles. As for the "sailor," he was smoking and looking at a colour catalogue. With dyed hair samples hanging down between the pages. After a minute, Jess said (Lydia could imagine the lips forming prettily, detracting from the slightly masculine chin):

"I've got Chan working for me tomorrow so I can go to the Green demo."

In the corner of Lydia's eye, the sailor looked up, smiling sweetly (he had a dimple in his chin).

Silence. The sailor adding: "Those magenta ex-extensions finally came in. F-fab colour."

Lydia sat still. As if in a dream, with two "Norma jeans." (In a sense there are thousands, "real" or facsimile, on postcards, on streets, in boutiques and beauty salons.) Or, conversely, that woman from Toronto could be a split personality, ephemeral in the shadows of her being. If so, how did this funkier half live? Did she also have a white apartment? Or something darker, black walls and silver paper bunched along the roof. Did she have a cat? Would she (as Lydia was sure any woman with a lost cat would eventually) cast a spell to draw it back? First you light a candle. Then carefully pull towards yourself a piece of paper tied with string on which you've written: *Tink, Tink, come back if you want to.* The caveat's important. She knew the cat was alive. Having met it one night suddenly in the alley. The cat, terrified, flying over backyard fences six feet high to get away. That cat could do incredible things with its body. Adopting all the cat's-cradles positions possible on the sofa. "Arms" crossed, apart, back, little triangular nose down and forward. However, she feared its powers of observation. Ses prunelles full of light staring staring. A cat could in one glance strip you of the suburban ©, or any other, that mothers try to stamp upon their daughters from the time they're little. For their self-protection. The mother brushing brushing with the silver brush from the shiny end-table. Stroking. Kissing. Cuddling to make the little girl feel perfect. Which couldn't cover up the feeling of something terribly wrong.

Lydia looked up: above her head a stuffed owl watched silently.

The only other thing to report, from reality, was that Theresa, from the choir of Santa Cruz, the Portuguese church with lit-up fluorescent bouquets on its white stucco front, suddenly sang a high note. Illustrating how sublime it is to be soprano.

Lydia disregarded the owl (of all birds, the owl was most like her) and wrote (painfully) on the placemat, a line from another dream she'd had: *People taking birds in*

*their hand. Me objecting because not everybody knows how to*
*hold a baby bird—*

*10.* On St. Patrick's Day, Lydia came in shaking off the
weather. So nondescript as to be … effectively indescrib-
able. Inside, the place all decked in green. Green beer in
the glasses. Also green were the bread rolls served with the
meals. She chose a chair carefully at an angle, not to see
the stuffed birds and animals perched along the walls.
This time the "true" Norma jean was there (only two
tables over). Looking once more different (the woman was
evolving!). In tweed jacket, jodhpur-style pants, peaked
cap, nicely fitting sweater whose colour reflected a thread
in the jacket. In fact, every colour-detail matching every
other. "To the point of anal," thought Lydia. A little envious of the quality of N.j.'s female companion: obviously a
dancer in print silk skirt, very muscled legs in good black
tights with a seam up the back and nice little boots. To
whom Norma jean was desperately trying to speak French.
"Ouiii, la mohde, maiy …" Then switching to English to
make her point. "Sure style's everything in art. But don't
you think it's important to somehow represent social
notions, like race, class?"

"Ou bien," the woman replied, provocatively,
"comme l'indépendance du Québec?"

Lydia nearly laughed. Wiping with effort the smirk
off her face. To concentrate on her placemat, the writing
of her dream. Another *Bird Dream,* in fact. She picked up
her pen, noting (in the corner of her eye) that Norma jean
had glanced over. While saying loudly, earnestly, to the

dancer that every national minority should be represented equally in the main government institutions and culture-producing groups. This made the Québécoise angry. Norma jean added humbly she maybe wasn't living enough yet in French to understand the nuances. "If I'm going to get anywhere, I have to learn the French they speak here."

"You have to learn French, period, sweetheart," said Lydia. Trying to think of an appropriate line from *Donkey Riding*. While taking stock of N.j.'s hypocritical English way of pretending to be polite when the mat gets yanked out from underneath your feet. Gently touching the dancer's arm. Who (surprisingly) returned the favour. Was it possible the two of them were friends?

A nerve twitched on Lydia's elegant cheek. She wrote, taking care to make the *I*'s big and swarthy (a sign the ego is intact): *My father and mother and some others taking baby birds in their hands (me not objecting to my mother so much as to the others). Of course I kind of want to pick them up too. There seems to be an unusually close relationship in this dream between animals and people. Looking around in this kind of garden we're in, I notice several people—children I think, in part—in a tree, perched on branches as if they were birds too. I do the same, sitting on the very top of a tree with a very smooth trunk and hardly any branches.*

Lydia stopped writing. Her head inexplicably burgeoning as if a big turd were pressing on the top. Like at the osteopath's, involving some reference to her father. His weak lips only trembling as he bathed her. A man afraid to ask for what he wanted. Unlike Ralph, whose gnarled hands were pounding more and more impatiently on the table. Making the war medals pinned to the jacket he wore over his old sailor's twisted-with-arthritis body tinkle loudly. Finally staggering to his feet. Weaving as if his skinny, bowed legs were planted on some stormy deck. "Annie," he called, giggling and pointing sheepishly to his glass: "It's empty."

Lydia looked at Norma jean. Who was trying to change the subject of conversation before she made another gaffe: "I had a nightmare," she said, unconsciously cupping her large breast in her hand. While the dancer took in every word (and gesture). Probably pretending to be mesmerized in order to get her dance troupe on a tour of English Canada. Lydia smiled mockingly. Busily writing the rest of her dream: *Suddenly I have to get down from the tree covered with bird-children in a hurry. Looking at the slim branchless smooth erected trunk I'm sure that I will die. The trunk is very smooth and hard, a kind of reddish brown. But I slide down somehow (with an umbrella?) and feel victorious. However, there's trouble in the house. Which is an old wooden structure, possibly made of logs, with pine-slatted floors. And a separate entrance for the public. I can't remember what I might have done wrong.*

N.j.'s companion said in broken English: "Night Mare. Your nights are full of mares. I like thees Eenglish word." Norma jean smiling slightly sadly: "Except I dreamed I shot my mother." (On the tape deck Bob Marley was singing *I Shot the Sheriff.*) Adding with a wistful grin on her face: "But I didn't shoot her deputy."

Unfortunately, at that precise moment, the waitress whizzed by Lydia's table. Her hand holding high a tray with a glass of something red. In the direction of Ralph. The better to shut him up. The corner of her apron catching Lydia's placemat. Which flew through the air, aided by some draft. Landing at Norma jean's feet. Who leaned over (not before glancing ironically at Lydia) and picked the paper up.

Perhaps she didn't really see Norma jean walking towards her. Norma jean standing at her table. Looking at her through green eyes set in white white skin, a tiny unpretentious mole above her pretty lips.

"You think you're so tough," said N.j., waving the placemat in the air. "You don't even have the guts to call this dream what it really is:

*"The Perfect Incest Dream."*

**(the sky is what I want)**

The bar. Multiple empty chairs. All the regulars departed
—not counting Ralph, making more and more noise. Plus
certain occasional clients still hoping for human contact
(i.e., to pick someone up). Under the smell of smoke,
odours of food, alcohol—their pungent perfumes, anxious
sweat, vaguely awakened sexes: people labouring very hard
on intimate or existential questions. Heads turned to the
side, talking, talking, with small frowns between the eyebrows. Then laughing loudly. Or sitting by themselves
quietly brooding.

Getting hardly any answers.

Lydia lights a cigarette (trembling a little). Looking
out towards the roofs, gaily trimmed in readiness for a
party of her "brides." Including Lydia (the portrait).

Which persona's now gathering her defences against any over-dramatization of effects of possible past events that might come up. Not believing in causality any more than in the cacophony of statistics. Being only an ordinary woman, with the average experience of growing up (i.e., a good chance of, uh, harm). But people take things differently. "You just have to digest what happens to you," an astrologer told her once.

"Exactly," thinks Lydia, gently listing forward. Foot tapping on the floor to something like a tango. Flashing on that warm, secure feeling she had walking into the astrologer's office last winter. Shiny black table. In the centre of the room, a computer with a brightly coloured chart of moons, stars, magnetic lines, meridians. Beyond a window, a white winter sky. Hanging low over pressed-metal reliefs on flat grey buildings from a later period (therefore plain squares and circles) than those on The Main. Stretching out in a north-easterly direction towards an empty white horizon. The astrologer, thin, with blue eyeshadow on her hooded eyelids (a Scorpio for sure), said (kindly, like an aunt): "Vénus in Cancer. La peur de perdre en amour. You have to *open* yourself a little."

Lydia's voice rose as high as a girl's, asking if the chart indicated any, uh, weird experience, young.

"My job's the future," the astrologer retorted, turning her birdlike head towards the screen. "Ne rien exagérer. What you're speaking of n'est pas comme un, a, a concentration camp. *Bien sûr, il faut la digérer.*"

In the bar, the tango music stops. Lydia orders brandy (the very last one), plus water. Toe suspended impatiently underneath the table. Eyes vaguely on a poster hanging by the door. At first glance, a tourist ad for the Dominican Republic. Yellow sun sinking in black sky, on black-and-white water. She tries to read the caption: DERRIÈRE LES PLAGES ... 500,000 HAÏTIENS Y SONT TRAITÉS COMME LES ESCLA——

But it's shadowed by a woman, faded skirt, faded brown hair, heavy shoes on her feet, possibly a street person, entering the bar. The woman picks a table. Looking around, commandingly, expectantly. When the waitress doesn't come, she begins talking very loudly:

"My mother said: 'You're a whore.'"

"I said: 'Okay, Mom, if that's what you want.'"

"On this subject, Leonard Cohen owes me money."

Lydia's head feels tight. Also, paradoxically, as if on the verge of exploding into euphoric little bubbles. Kind of like blacking out. "I should say—like dissolving into essence," she thinks, straightening, looking at her hand (for no apparent reason). "An essence, escaping into air. Making love to the city. Tasting, sucking, smelling, like a real (male?) poet." No. An essence is ephemeral, therefore not "male" or "female" or any of the watchwords in media and politics: Good. Bad. Man. White. Black. Feminist. Incest survivor. Victim. If only History (the kind she's waiting for) could be like this fluid thing she's thinking of: smooth and gently moving (her hand makes a wavy motion in the air). Full of nuance, broad, accessible, instead of mean and categorical. Of course, everyone would have to have the same (material) capacity for existence. For not getting murdered—

At the word "murdered" Lydia drains her glass. Because, conjuring up once more that scene in the park. The green green grass so innocent in the dawn. She, Lydia, high on fasting, almost floating on it. Until she tripped—over a girl's leg, sticking out from underneath a bush. Immediately retreating to a distant bench for purposes of observation. The air around white and still as if time had locked. Sooner or later: the cops. With their blanket. Next came the mother: cheap flowered dress, a dash of lipstick, comb hastily pulled through her hair in readiness for a drama she still couldn't believe she was part of. Then, naturally, the media (not television, the story wasn't big—the "girl" just a small-time hooker with some lousy pimp who wouldn't give out her address). The mother's voice fake-cheerful in order to keep control—

Lydia shakes her head. It's 12:55. On the airwaves (some local radio station), the barely audible late-night news. Trouble brewing in the community of Oka—due to a golf course being extended onto sacred Mohawk ground. Serious lack of rain. Several dépanneur robberies. The murder in the park this morning. The (woman) announcer's voice pauses, as if departing from the script. "The third murder of a young woman in as many months. But the police see no connection."

Lydia grabs her placemat and writes something down. Not the names of women going through her head: Jo, Chantal, Anne-Marie, Heidi. But a list of sayings. A game she plays with herself when nothing else is happening.

   *1. I nearly died laughing.*

   *2. . . . . . .*

## Night Music

### (3 Scenes in 4 Acts)

### *ACT I*

It's late. The crowd in the bar's thinning out. The waitress turns up the community radio station. A beautiful husky voice says (in the official and unofficial languages): "Bonjour, les amies. Time for a little night music." Lydia looks up expectantly. She knows that voice.

"Welcome to our program. And for all you spurned lovers out there, a tune called *Jealousy*." Lydia shuts her eyes in pure pleasure. Remembering (in a rush of sentiment) the voice's generous mouth. Shiny red hair. Handwriting like little birds' tracks. The women around her all small, too. With small bones in their men's shirts raised high at the collar. Their names, as musical as birdsongs. Small tough fingers. The skin (Lydia thinks) of people who glow, because they do exactly what they want.

Cello's brow, especially, made her think of freedom. A clear, high brow. Moving suddenly from the hot streets of Montréal where, in summer, women cast large shadows (in neutral winter light, almost none). To an ochre adobe house on the desert in Georgia O'Keeffe land. A small oasis fed by sluices opened weekly. Flooding quince, pear, peach, fig, apple, lemon flower so sweet. Loose lemon-grass with tarantulas, scorpions, roaches fleeing before the flood (some, in the direction of the house). The garden, an air of innocence (despite wildly singing birds) sur-rounded by a village surrounded by a desert. From which at dusk owls, bobcats, mule deer, lizards emerged. Cello, a naturalist, was said to have unusual communication with these animals. Especially the wide-eyed mule deer. Who probably liked her way of standing back and watching. Totally non-judgemental. Never angrily squeezing little furry collars.

The free-floating type.

Lydia laughs: so free-floating her voice down there in the desert's still floating out from this radio station in Montréal. Probably a replay. Lydia thinks of the commu-nity radio station's crooked green steps farther up The Main. Leading to the slanted room they called the studio. Lined with old green felt. Minimal technology. An ante-room with chairs of peeling lacquered wood curved over iron legs, from some church basement. She closes her eyes in mock religious fervour (better than going home and fac-ing her empty room). Seeing a stamped-earth courtyard and horizontal stripes (a half-open shutter). A stage-set maybe. That old rococo-style theatre where Cello, Bruca, Montana, did a performance called *Deliquescence*. In which the basic movement was a tango that kept dissolving into a triangle. But the love triangle must have been a foil, a metaphor for something. Lydia smiles crookedly, remembering: the music suspended for a minute. The small hands of C. and B. touching each other's faces. In a light-yet-lingering connection concocted for the theatre. With M. standing tall, skinny, almost cowboy-like, in the shadow: watching. Behind her, in turn, an old black-and-white picture of a young woman on a horse. The woman in the picture had prim Victorian curls—a joking contrast to the boldness of her carriage, the wildness of her eyes. In front of her, M. smiling, smiling ironically, mysteriously. At the two women "kissing." Then one of them was holding M. The other having dissolved into the background. The passion mostly in the way a hand grasped an arm, the bend of a knee.

"Je vous offre," says Cello's tart, rich voice across the airwaves of the bar. "Je vous offre un tango. The dance of death and love."

Probably Bruca was the lead bird. She didn't appear it, being tiny, nervous. Probably, she choreographed that small group of stage-hands, musicians, dancers, artists in their men's shirts buttoned to the top, over which perfect short haircuts revealed delicious pink napes. Preparing for their performance in the pseudo-rococo theatre, which their presence filled (at least for Lydia) with fascinating, hereto unknown sensations. Women parting in their forever dissolving tango. *Comme si aucun couple ne pouvait tenir le coup* (it said, mock-dramatic) in the program. M. watching, then leaning over B., leaning back under her. Theatrically exaggerating the gesture. Their sexes almost touching in the famous moment of suspension allegedly perfected in the brothels of Argentina.

"Chères auditrices," says Cello's voice, teasingly on the radio. "Je vous embrasse toutes ..."

Lydia thinks of her sitting in the radio station, grinning, with the big old-fashioned earphones. Outside the door that empty row of chairs in the studio ante-room. It's raining.

"Et maintenant, voici Paola Sola, singing ..."

The scene cuts to an early winter street. Two a.m. A woman walking on it. Happy (sad) angry. For the banal reason that her lover's lying to her. Walking, raincoat collar up, the woman tries to grasp the movement of her feelings. To understand why gloating happiness— no—satisfaction, at the knowledge of a lover's betrayal, always gives way to panic. She was getting bored with that cowgirl anyway. Furthermore (the walking woman thinks), her lover's stupid infatuation shows such a lapse of taste, it throws worse light on the betrayer than on the betrayed. Leaving the impression her lover would settle for anything ...

The wind blows a bleak sheet of rain in the woman's face. A sagging arcade door opens. A group of youths emerging clad in black, dark eye-circles. One crying: "Je ne veux pas m'en aller sans mon boss, où est-ce qu'il est, mon boss?" Like a child, almost. The pale, ragged female adolescents adopting looks of tolerance. The woman thinks: no use going home. At least when walking she feels happy or else angry. But the minute she lies down, starts dropping off to sleep—— sucked back into a sadness quickly-becoming-terror. As if to sleep would be to die. Precisely at the moment the body sinks in sleep, this starts, this panic rising from the stomach, waking her again. No amount of self-willed struggling resis resis-tance seems to stop it. As long as conscious, she can maintain order in her mind. But at the point where wake concedes to sleep, that inner voice she's fighting to keep down, with such plucky determination, surfaces, crying: "I'm betrayed, I'm abandoned."

"Ce tango est dédié aux filles du 6 décembre." Cello's voice grave.

Silence. (In the bar, three female clients, separately, get an image of 14 silver coffins on icy white snow.)

"Nous autres, on continue à vivre."

The woman walks faster, followed by a man. Cultivating anger. Angry at her exhaustion. Angry because of how she undertook in good faith the fight to keep despair at bay. Thinking she could do it. (The creep's talk-ing to her.) Thinking she could deal with this situation smoothly. Without some past forgotten trauma pop pop-ping up to stop her. Not that trauma ever pops up dir-ectly. Just the fear attached to it. As if anything were simple. Yes, it's exactly at the moment of losing conscious-ness in sleep that the terror always hits. ("O, tu n'aimes pas les gars," the creep says, walking right beside her.) Night after night until the fear of sinking into a place (sleep) so vulnerable, unprotected from that incessant inner voice, saying "Now you've done it, now you've done it, now you've lost her due to your own stupidity," drives you crazy. So you can't do it any more, go to bed. "Tu as raison. Si j'étais une femme, je serais comme ça," the creep adds, speeding up to pass.

But this is off the track. Lydia looks around the bar. Suddenly feeling good. The women's profiles here so beautiful (the few that are left): red, blonde, brunette. Close at a table, in intimate conversation, or looking sideways, like on ancient Greek engravings. Crete, or that woman-inhabited island devoted to cultivating the spirit of Aphrodite, Artemis and Charis (music, poetry, love). Of course, *then* life and art seemed one. The tango (on the other hand) so obsequiously the creation of illusion. Un pied qui marche de côté: side-step over fear, desire. Forward collés. The degree of physical contact projected by the audience. Who, eyes drawn by moving light caressing the abundant nooks and crannies in the old rococo theatre, also thought they saw images of women in trouble with reality (the law). Their images superimposed on images of wide-winged angels, lush fruit, brightly hued birds, painted on the theatre wall: girls with guns. Girls on horses (magnificent steeds). Different generations. In cocked hats. Shiny chins. Flapper haircuts. Blue-rimmed glasses. All staring at the camera with that look rebellious women have.

"The tango," says Cello, on the radio, "is incomparably sensual, though the sexes rarely touch. Like lesbians," she laughs.

The walking woman stops, seeing a cop car on that drizzly November street: a perfect video image.

Lydia thinks: "I'm confusing art with real. I'll have to unwind the thread—." But she feels resentful. Maybe at the trompe-l'oeil effect in everything they did. Perpetually covering grey with boldness, never losing face. Still, a certain nostalgia leaked through. In Bruca's almost flapper way of dressing, Cello's connection with the desert, Montana's name and allure. Hearkening always towards elsewhere, like the effusive decorations on the late-Victorian architecture up and down this street. Or like in old-fashioned stereoscope images where the second frame disrupts the content of the first. In the trio's performance, too, the notion of displacement: the play of lights and shadows over horsewomen, dancers partly disguised as men (with a flash of lace corset under an open jacket), serpents, the sexual ambivalence of angels, causing a perpetual restlessness of the eye. Luring the audience to identify with a certain kind of dream that no one could live up to (Lydia remembers thinking). A Utopic ambivalence, underscored in the program distributed at the door (by a very cute dyke with short brown hair, one gold earring and red ruffled chintz pulled tight at the waist). Or maybe it was her first glowing view of them that caused her to read something deeper than really meant into the program's caveat: *This is not a melodramatic triangle. But high romanticism. Up to you, chères spectatrices, to see the difference.*

"Chères auditrices ... *jalouses*," says Cello's voice over the airwaves. "Je vous embrasse le sexe. There, do you feel better now?"

Lydia remembers the ante-room next to the radio station studio. From which Cello, one night, seemed to vanish. Showing up later in her lush desert garden. The ante-room, painted black for some reason. Black with that row of empty chairs. As far as she knows no woman has ever been hassled doing a program late at night. Despite the paint-chipped, badly fitting door often swinging open into the dark, slowly emptying street.

The walking woman (she could also be a memory) wonders what four cop cars, all empty, are doing parked by a pharmacy in the middle of the night. Beyond which, some warehouses. The slick street zooming in a ribbon towards a place called Le Cake. The green-domed Le Lux. Between the two, a swinging door leading up the stairs to the grimy studio from which, over the airwaves, the notes of a Paola Sola tango swish and bend languidly.

"*Face it!*" thinks Lydia, "it was my voyeuristic side that wanted absolutely to reduce the 'deliquescence' of their tango to a mere love-triangle ..." Whereas, in reality (it said so in the program) its meaning was something else: the figures, demi-lune, assise, flexion, glissade, déhanchement, galop, danced by three, were elements in a field where any preference was permitted. As long as non-judgemental. Lydia glances around at the thinning group of clients nodding quietly over drinks. Lulled, maybe, by the resonance of Cello's voice. Cool crescent smile opening over cheeky small teeth (which no one could see, the studio and its ante-room always empty at this time of night). Herself, a little Grecian with the smooth cap of bright hair and charming curve of sandal. Totally assertive. Claiming to be overwhelmed sometimes by how many women in a room she could make love to. That posturing bugged Lydia. The whole gang was like that. Smart-ass, exclusive—yet inspiring.

"L'après-jalousie ..." Cello's whispering voice fading off, ironically seductive due to the little laugh behind it.

Offering them now a tenor sax's sweet high notes, suddenly breaking into a melancholic cry in the heat of the bar. Increasingly subdued.

Out the bar window a couple passes. His tanned, square-fingered hand roughly grasping the fine material of her blouse around her waist.

The walking woman, tired of waiting for action—cops or drug-store robbers to distract her from her inner melodrama, steps forward. Sticking to the main streets at three a.m. isn't dangerous. She can protect herself. She could try once more to sleep. Or walk the quadrangle again. Along Mont-Royal est. Past those old houses with sagging roofs once inhabited by workers of the shale pits, now arcades for French, English, Latino kids. A peep show. A strip joint. Empty restaurants selling empanadas, spaghetti, banana splits. Right down St-Denis below the university, to Ste-Catherine. Past that hotel where, in alleys, hookers wait. And where once in an upstairs room the walking woman actually peed her pants when a would-be lover came at her. Growing stains on bright-red jeans.

She steps forward, away from the cop cars. The sadness is a trope. She *wants* to leave her lover. It's only natural to be terrified of no more sex or small complicities. So close to the end of this unsatisfactory century. Especially—if someone else is kissing (that cowgirl's) pink lips.


*ACT II*

Lydia frowns. That woman was a subtext. Or maybe a projection. On a video screen pulled half-over a painted winged horse in the large middle grotto of the theatre wall. She'll have to wind deeper. To that flat where she first met the three of them: Montana, Cello, Bruca. A flat at the back of a grassy courtyard. In a leaning building reached by crooked steps behind a square-arched opening, with, at its corners, two minaret-shaped turrets. Lydia walked through. Zigzagging over the black-and-grey squares of the long walk behind her tall friend, the architectural historian. Her heart beating in anticipatory excitement because he said, turning (with almost priestly lisp):

"You're going to like this.

"I suggest you-you contrive to invite them for dinner."

What struck immediately was the slant of the floor. Green-painted hardwood lurching down towards the north-east corner. She loved the idea of women living in a place with the bottom falling out. The main room whitewashed and covered with mostly natural objects: relics, and living animals and plants. A large fish-skull print, painted bright mint. In a wet dish, the grasping lips of a fly-catching plant. The end-table was Cello's contribution: little blue fluorescent desert beetles in a low case, climbing over sand on high spindly legs. Struggling little tacks. Beyond the casement window, the visitor could see the Italianate domes of L'Église St-Jean Baptiste. Gulls swooping low towards it in the mottled sky.

"Vous êtes jalouses, chères auditrices, because you're afraid what people think. Social structures." Cello's husky voice, rasping, tense or, possibly, swollen with laughter. Under the headphones in the studio, her green, brown-flecked eyes.

(At the bottom of the stairs the green-chipped door springs open.)

Lydia's eyes close. Imagining C.'s smile, her cheeky teeth with the space between them. She can still totally relish the sensation of that first time, walking through the arch with her friend towards the leaning stairs. The damp, softening spring earth already making her feel sensual. Blinking at the sudden brightness of the light as she entered their flat. Sitting, unbidden, at the table. Practically in a trance. A ray of light cutting Bruca's small hand holding a cigarette. Bruca's bright-red lips twittering in mockery of Lydia's awkwardness as she spoke. "And you are ... *who?*" Cello's direct magnetic gaze: an unfamiliar combination of tenderness and hardness. Both of them flirting with her. Montana's tall skinny shadow suddenly darkening the door. Cooking steak in the background. Her head turning left over a broad shoulder to look at them from time to time. On the table, some sketches and photos of that old theatre, farther up Park Avenue. With its façade of garlanded masks, oeils-de-boeuf and little gargoyles reaching straight up towards the sky from the parapet. In one of the oeils-de-boeuf, someone had inserted (some old ad campaign) a picture of a well-built man in clinging yellow bathing briefs.

"Oh, cute," said her friend, the architectural historian: "Rococo pretensions. What could be more redundant?" His profile, hair drawn back but not too tightly over the long, long neck, studied attentively the festooned recesses with cherubs or angels painted in them, plush seats, curve of balcony. Lydia looked too. Wondering if she should ask if rococo, as a backdrop for their performance, was intended as a metaphor. (An annoying Henry James line was tickling her mind: *Miss Osmond, indeed, in the bloom of her juvenility, had a touch of the rococo.*)

She unwinds the thread farther: Montana. The deep points of her cowboy-shirt collar tipped in leather. Bruca, smoking a cigarette and taking it all in. The ultra-confident type who could synthesize a situation (Lydia attributed this to the fact she came from money) and decide on a move in one simple glance. Impossible to remember what she wore —except the bright-red, gently mocking lips. She knows she stared at Cello, but, with the stunned obstinacy of first attraction, remembers only Cello's high brow and smooth cap of (naturally) near-orange hair. Nothing rococo, that is, antiquated or overdecorated, about them.

Outside the rain has nearly stopped.

That couple again passes by the window, the guy holding in his large hand the woman's tiny waist. Organdy, no doubt. Almost as if dancing—but not quite Argentinian style, that saucy march where the movement of the leg is carried by the hip. The dancers' shoulders square, ritualistically formal, challenging each other. Danced originally, it's said, on the stamped earth of abattoirs by men in couples, nostalgic for the muslin waists of women. For the handle of a knife. Or by gauchos and women paid to tango with them: une danse sans paroles pour couples bien enlacés. Cheeks always parallel, the march movement coupled with a déhanchement reminiscent of Africa.

*On le dansait avec les pauses.*

The rain has stopped completely.

The walking woman passes the fake Doric columns climbing the glass façade of a renovated warehouse. Faster, to block out her lover's pink lips. The word "lesbian" feeling suddenly less ambivalent. She wants to be one completely. Instead of pretending she could easily go elsewhere. Because, oh, the softness of a woman's stomach when you put your face against it ... This (by extension) reminding her how much she wants to taste her lover's sex. Especially that incomparably erotic moment when the tongue perceives the body starting its vibrations. Before the avalanche. She'd always done a lot of holding back (which she's starting to regret). Chiefly—that cowgirl was trying to treat her like a wife.

The waitress approaches Lydia's table.

She can still see herself, that first time. Sitting in their flat, wanting to adore them. Especially, the strange brown-flecked eyes of Cello. Out of shyness, she looked instead at Montana, leaning on the counter. Already growing muscles. Eating steak from the restaurant of her father (a former hockey star)—dark-lacquered, cigar-smelling, many banquet-rooms. The bulge of Montana's arm impressive, when she suddenly grabbed Lydia and led her sweetly in a one-two one-two one-pause ... around the table. Though it was clear that Lydia wanted Cello. Montana's shoulders as broad as a man's under the cropped blonde hair. Was she taking drugs or, more likely, homeopathic "remedies" to improve her body mass? It was said

Montana would do anything for Bruca, Cello, she loved them both so much. Lydia winces, remembering, on stage, Montana in a single continuous movement disentangling her thigh from Cello's, half-turning (Bruca stepping in), and flying through the air. Horizontal to the floor. Long taut body in striped pants, black vest flying back to reveal lace halter-top. Breath in small short gasps, her torso visibly heaving in its lace over the almost completely flat chest.

The walking woman passes the swinging door of the radio station on the upper Main. The door swings open twice, and shut again.

"Take me back," Lydia had entreated. Following her friend the architectural historian's elegant slender form out across the dampness of the courtyard. Which smelled of cat piss in certain corners on which the sun never shone. He swung his long hair over his shoulders and looked at her provocatively.

"*Love Is a Many Splendored Thing*," C.'s voice says, filling up the bar. Teasing.

"Sure," smirks Lydia. Imagining C.'s tiny mole over the right side of the pink lips as she spoke into the mike. Offering her listeners, now, another danse du poignard (so named by a certain Mr. Borges). She only wishes C.'s group of many splendours were in the radio studio with her (the door downstairs once more creaks open). Sitting in the ante-room waiting for her to finish. Their charming heads visible through the large plate-glass window, behind which Cello sat, pushing buttons, carefully setting needles on old scratched vinyl: Montana's cropped head, Bruca's gold curls; the stage-hands, Irène, shy, freckled;

Zoe, jutting chin, fine mouth, flying-back hair (resembling the falcon of a disappearing species she claimed had made its perch outside her window). Nothing rococo about them—except maybe their exquisite relationship to the plant and animal world. Making it a point of honour, like animals, not to bother others with the trope of sadness.

"Last call," says the waitress, impatient, close to Lydia's table.

On the radio, now, a tango called *Margot*. Oh—they were playing that song (about a kept girl from some outskirt slum, whose new-found finery could not hide the hunger in her eyes) the night Lydia walked into the old rococo theatre. Full of hope and desire. Because, engraved on her mind, the five pairs of eyes (Zoe and Irène must have been there, too), bold, challenging around the table, when she'd walked into their flat. Waiting (Lydia felt) to see if she were good enough. In the theatre, she passed through the glassed-in lobby. Took a program from the cute dyke at the second set of doors. Cello, stage director, sitting right on stage at a sepia-painted table. Watching Bruca and Montana. Music. Pause. A right foot describing a slight arc towards the centre, its toe grazing, in passing, the left heel … In the tango, it is the man who moves forward, after a single step in retreat, the better to keep his eye on the door.

Lydia remembers (the waitress's trying to say something) sitting on a worn plush seat next to centre aisle. Reading in the program (she wondered if the message weren't too obvious): *Originally, dancing the tango, with its mix of nostalgia, anger, ironic eye turned in on despair, represented an act of rebellion.* Later—progressing from the suburbs of Montevideo and Buenos Aires to downtown clubs, the dance grew sentimental. Ruined by the time it got to Europe. Sitting there, she hungrily drank in what was happening on the stage (practically nothing) as if it were their lives. According to the gossip. Their capacity for work, plus legendary love affairs: especially Cello, who loved many, loving especially Bruca, tiny, shell-like with her bright blonde curls; Bruca, it was thought, favouring Montana.

Is that why Cello left? Does she have any of them with her now in her ochre adobe house? One white room, a low bed with a Mexican blanket on it. In which also live a lizard, a puppy, a large cat with curved claws, a tarantula in the frame of the door. Then Cello's current house guest enters—feeling instantly that she's interrupting a highly intimate moment. Cello laughs, and takes her by the hand. Soon (Lydia likes to think) they're driving over a secluded stretch of bone-white sand. Scarlet sunset with flat turquoise clouds. Beyond 400 miles of gently rolling dunes, sites where nuclear blasts happened in the 50s. (The army occupies a large chunk of the state.) Lydia's lips pass (in her mind) over the large curved nipples of the breasts, the stomach. Salty sand underneath.

"You're jealous, girls, because you live too much for love."

The walking woman turns right and heads along Mont-Royal est in the rain. Even this slummy street is changing (and *she'll* change, too): second-hand shops as if in Soho. Bars, arcades, under the sagging roofs of 19th-century houses, originally built for coal haulers living at the edge of the city. Healthy drug trade. She herself never much needed anything like that. Except when losing. Then—it's her impression—so needy as to terrify. Example: the other day, sitting, distant, cool, by her (ex-) lover, whom she'd met in some café. Yet her body (le corps a ses raisons) drifting drifting over, until snuggling close, every pore alive. Wanting to kiss her so much she was going crazy. At the same time, feeling self-betrayal.

Lydia grasps harder at the thread. Probably this scene in the theatre was the rehearsal. Where she went with her friend the architectural historian. A red plush curtain. A huge popcorn machine (later removed). On the wall, a blow-up image of a woman in cowboy hat and boots looking at a large Bible, open to a lily, in a jewellery-store window. Suddenly Cello, sitting at her brown table, in brown pinstriped suit, shoes with spats, blushed to the roots of her hair. As if, in concentrating on the movement of Montana in a tux, dancing with Bruca, the latter's hair combed behind her tiny ears, small bones, delicate yet tough with the healthy wiry thinness, perfect posture of certain women who know who they are, as if, in seeing the way their shoulders spoke aggressively, yet tenderly, to each other, or the brushing of a thigh—she, Cello, saw something she'd never seen before. Her strong hand fumbled nervously with a pencil on the table. Behind which, rough stairs climbed from the stage into various dark corners. Occasionally brightened by a swinging light, the panting stamen in the wide-open lily (magnified with mirrors), or a detail of the theatre's original decor: curve of a bird's massive wing (it could also be an angel).

The walking woman walks east on Mont-Royal. Not noticing that creep who was trying to talk to her has again dropped behind.

"Nous autres [C.'s voice again filling up the bar], on continue à vivre. Jealousy's a privilege."

"Yeah," thinks Lydia, remembering watching Cello watch Montana pulling Bruca close: the moment of suspension in that particular dance when anything can happen. Lydia, watching the pain in Cello's eyes with a certain satisfaction. As the inner and outer thighs of the dancers joined. Bruca leading, brash, aggressive; Montana, following, relaxed, body completely disposed to the press of the guiding hand on the small of the back. Then suddenly taking over. Cello's chin raised, green eyes in pale face looking right and left in case, maybe, anyone had noticed her discomfort. Then jumping up and clapping. A small smile flushing through the slowly, relaxing, body falling back into the chipped-turquoise chair. "Perfectly executed, my dear," said Lydia's tall friend, the architectural historian. Looking at Cello, not the dancers.

The walking woman steps past a bar with a guy singing French country-music. Past run-down shops in darkness. Trying to walk briskly. Trying to focus on the loneliness, unhappiness she always felt with that cowgirl. The surge of relief at the point of parting. So why her pain so palpable that, sitting on the balcony of a friend, looking past some low houses, the top of the club called Crocodile, towards the lights of the soccer field, she felt at the edge of where being and nothingness join? Every sensation (now the cries of the soccer players) outlined with a clarity, a light indicating the blessedness of this state. If the body could take it—

*ACT III*

"Ça fait une bonne demi-heure que je dis last call," the waitress says to Lydia.

*Effectivement,* in the bar the chairs are nearly empty.

Lydia only wishes that in that ante-room of that studio on the upper Main the chairs weren't empty too (the door swinging open).

She grasps tighter at the thread (starting to feel impatient): if Cello left, took off to the desert, she must have had a reason. Professional? Or romantic? Lydia's mind (due to alcohol) keeps slipping towards the latter. Although she knows there's something deeper. *Whom* did Cello love? Bruca, small, pretty, possibly manipulative (using self-denial, some said, to create dependency in others). Her words, few, though precise, mocking if you happened to be a stranger. Which words, in a show of honour, could get turned back, like stagelights, towards herself. In love, drawing herself up and being understanding of the "betrayer." Of course she didn't see it that way, which made it possible for her to do it. To construct herself like that.

Cello was the opposite: earthy, extroverted, always pursuing someone. Probably (Lydia smiles wanly) had huge ejaculations. But, sometimes she wondered (that strain of bitterness again) if Cello's aura of special communicative powers with desert plants and animals wasn't also a construction. The construction of a comfortable American, trained at nature schools and summer camps (of course, you have to have it in you). Sitting in the ochre adobe house (after she left the city) with several pets around her. In her loose brown shift. Pulled a little high on the brown thighs for the comfort of the house guest. Outside, the opened sluices starting to flood the garden.

But Lydia can transform ambivalence immediately to elation with yet another drink. She tells this to the waitress.

The walking woman turns right on St-Denis: the street still sleek and shiny.

It's true, in the ochre adobe house, the quantity of insects made the house guest shiver. Brushing aside the cockroaches on the kitchen counter to make the coffee. Cello refused to kill them—they were only fleeing the irrigation water. Still, she, the guest, who rose to meet the morning before the others, felt joyful as she ground the coffee and put it in the pot with the long thin spout. Thinking how smart it was to come. Dawn and the incredible garden slowly waking up. Birds singing wildly. Including a scolding mockingbird very high up. At the table under the pecan tree, the fragrance from fruiting flowers enough to drive her crazy. Later, there'd be various people (mostly women) wandering in and out. She dwelled lovingly on the quality of the coffee and tobacco: this place could be anywhere in the world where people liked good things.

*I'd like to open some sluices. Yours* (said the postcard from her lover back home).

The "*yours*" seemed an afterthought. The guest passed over it (really wanting Cello).

Lydia laughs softly.

Another tango floats through the bar. Maybe *La morocha* (la brune); or *La rage du porteno*; or *Ce soir, ta peau sous la lune.* In their performance, the women danced cheek-to-cheek. Their arrogant profiles crossed or parallel; one leading with the right foot, the other with the left. The latter, traditionally the male, must never retreat from anything started. Exactly like a duel. The shoulders always facing. Each dancer, whether "dominant" or not, solidly in her space. Nostalgia leaking from every chord, gesture, for some thing, unsayable. Yet each instant standing out today, alone.

"Puis, mes jalouses, if you have your morocha by your side, just remember—she's not really yours."

The walking woman heads south on St-Denis. The scene is grey and black: her shadow on the slickness of the sidewalk. Past books in windows with learned titles, like *Dans l'oeil de l'aigle.* Past mannequins, antiques. Past the former junkie corner. Autumn always marks her failure to be cool. This has come up before, this feeling of breaking out of patterns. Getting wilder again. Standing free and confident on a corner of the street. Longing for the loneliness of a flat by the port. Instead of being corralled in by that cowgirl. Then the unconscious, in the form of a dream, leaks out around the edge of sleep, whispering: "You've been dumped."

On the slick street, the man behind moves closer.

Lydia grasps the thread once more: Cello, back when she taped the program in the radio station farther up the street. Small checks on her shirt. The greenness of her gaze! The uninvited guest noticed that same fervid look in the eyes of the several Southern, storytelling women sitting at her table. Under the fragrant pecan tree outside the ochre adobe house. The guest drew closer. A tiny female cop (red décolleté top) saying that her father (deaf) was digging fossils with his little girl in an old arroyo. Then a roar (heard only by her, but he trusted her when she told him). And boy, did they move fast: a huge wall of water rushing down the dry stream bed, where they'd been standing, from some storm in the mountains. In the desert, a storm could move that quickly. Another, called Santana, said there was an arroyo all right nearby where she worked. At a truckstop, where at night, the lot-lizards (women of the sex trade specializing in truckstops) went from truck to truck offering "grease jobs" and "window wipes." Wearing the usual tight pants, cut out at the crotch. "Sometimes," she said, "you can see their hair hanging down. We found one of them in the arroyo just before it filled."

"Stop pining [C.'s voice caressing]; you could always … kiss the girl beside you.

"Or else, pine, like a gaucho: with a little fight in you.

"Maintenant voici l'éternel Astor Piazzollo avec *Tango Très*."

The walking woman leans forward, hands in pockets. Right on rue Rachel. Under the mock-Italian domes of L'Église St-Jean Baptiste. Unaware of the guy following behind. Feeling angry that the effort of suppressing sadness (to be the kind of woman she wants—one who goes with changes) causes such rigidity of the body it's impossible to relax into sleep. She suddenly remembers two dykes in tight lace and lipstick kissing, extremely young and vibrant, on the cover of a magazine (making her want that cowgirl). This thought stirring her up so much she'll have to make another round, up The Main and down, across rue Mont-Royal, down St-Denis, cutting west by either Marie-Anne, Rachel or Duluth. Body leaning forward, every muscle taut.

Lydia grasps the thread tighter: the red plush curtains of the old rococo theatre. The antique jukebox-shaped popcorn machine (apparently judged excessive) pushed into a corner. Her ecstasy, almost, when the dancers, in a move, inadvertently displayed the characteristic stiffness of many North Americans (except Montana, the trained one in the group). Not abandoned to the movement in the trance state required by the dance. Abandoned, yet each one in a role: the "man," mythical, tough, explosive, yet restrained in his movements; the woman—qui, d'une voluptueuse agilité, exécute, soumise, les injonctions de son homme. Then—the effect of their simulated kiss (on lesbians always hungry for a public image): female hand on female cheek, the closeness of their lips. While behind, the light rested on a blow-up image of an arroyo with a woman on a horse riding out of it.

(There's a pause in the tape.)

In the bar, the waitress moves near a table where a woman's leaning over to try to kiss another. Whose head remains turned: the type who only waits.

Cello, also, only watched and waited. Sitting in her cool brown shift, encouraging the uninvited guest to tear herself away from the oasis-like garden. And explore the road north to Albuquerque: slim winding ribbon through army checkpoints, over deep arroyos, through villages with Mexican houses whose positioning flat against the sky recalled something of the Aztecs. The guest explaining (quickly) she preferred the freshness of the mornings at the table under the pecan tree. "If that's all right with you." Even if, sitting there at dawn, listening to the birds, a shiver ran up her spine, due to fear of scorpions (under the rock her sandalled foot had accidentally touched); or that dream she'd had last night. Titled *Un fait accompli.* Wherein she and her lover back in Montréal had already broken up (this would only happen later). The lover having left with some woman who had the initials of a province (she couldn't think *whom*). And she, the guest, running around an adobe courtyard in a panic. Trying to make a phone call from bilingual Spanish-English telephones. Noticing, though distraught, there was no posted language representing the aboriginal quarter of the state. The army's quarter, all fenced in and mined. Which was why, landing at the airport, the plane was full of colonels (shaved, meaty necks). Peering down at some launching pad or test-site for bombs.

Lydia looks around the bar at the remaining attractive women (tempted to create one more woman-on-the-roof). Hardly any men. People going home. Just outside the door, a group of Portuguese guys talking in their rhythmic argumentative English. Stars now vaguely visible in the sky beyond the pediments. She yawns, remembering the gossip. Cello leaving due to Bruca. Alternately, due to some incident in or near the radio studio, after taping a program. M. having found somebody new completely. The piano riff stops. But she'll have to stay till the end of the story: Montana, showing up surprisingly one night at the walking woman's door. So clean-smelling in her pressed man's shirt of very fine cotton. Plus the blush high on the cheekbone, a certain recklessness in her manner, making her ultimately seductive ...

The walking woman's going up The Main. Maybe slightly slower. Passing Miloud's, Crocodile, L'Empanada, Le Coin du Réfugié, etc. Every limb exhausted. But stubborn enough to focus on the bright side of things. That incredible sense of freedom at the end of love, of delicious solitude (a first defence—preceding deluge of pain). Biking across the city (from the shadows, a Somalian refugee extending a slim arm for money). Then the quality of light, sitting on that balcony looking west towards the ceramic-fronted Crocodile, the park, from which rose the cries of the overheated soccer players. Each object outlined as if it had an aura. Her tall friend standing there beside her (his voice a mixture of cynicism and concern): "In two weeks the hysteria will be over." A cop car passes; the refugee slips farther into the shadows.

The walking woman stops to light a cigarette, tall and handsome (a little slim, having completely lost her appetite). In her loose beige raincoat and short hair with flap over one ear.

The guy who's following slows down a little.

The waitress approaches Lydia's table. Outside, where the street, receding, becomes a thinner ribbon, the walking woman moves forward. Getting closer to the radio station door. The guy who's following looking more innocent now that a Walkman's stuck in his ear. There's a glitch in the tape. Lydia holds fast to the thread: "that proves nothing," she remembers thinking, that Cello left right after taping the show being replayed at this very moment. Followed, eventually, by the uninvited guest. The latter, feeling immediately she stepped off the plane (surrounded by colonels) as if she were on some American movie set. Desert everywhere, and sandstone cliffs with fissures, on whose sides lizards slept. Then, waiting up the street from Cello's, whose door was locked, in a Hawaiian-style bar. Happy, sitting there, on a terrace surrounded by a white plastic fence. Listening to some band of veterans play old country music. While white-haired couples gently did the two-step. Like in her grandmother's town much farther north. Thinking she needed *two* (Cello and her lover back in Canada) in order to feel good. Then, just as the sun suddenly slipped behind the horizon (kites flying high in the air), Cello came and got her. The two walking up the walk towards the ochre adobe house, the guest in white jeans, her hips swinging cheekily, confidently, in the breeze. This whole trip being an experiment in pushing things a little.

But Cello never so much as kissed her (and she wasn't the type to make the first move herself).

"*Entraineuse*," whispers C., announcing another tango.

The walking woman passes the radio station door.

*ACT IV*

The walking woman could have also been a figure passing in front of the old rococo theatre the night of their performance. Black and grey on the glistening sidewalk. Lydia (so elated), striding through the heavy carved doors, with their open glass transoms. The performance had no beginning. Comprised, only, of the trio dancing their deliquescent tango (while the audience came and went). Their high smooth cheeks, their bodies in men's dress with little feminine touches, catching something of the tango's original naughtiness: wanton, sardonic, ironic in despair. Cello, all in brown, occasionally cutting in from her brown table (beside which, in the shadows, sat some large brown animal). She the least natural of the three in men's clothing. Cutting in on Bruca, whose profile-of-a-moralist was held high with certitudes (belied by the blonde girlish curls). Also the endlessly moving lights: Irène, Zoe, firm, competent, in the light-booth behind the second balcony, giving the set an ephemeral quality. Caressing lace-encased breast, visible in the cleavage of a vest; the brushing of two thighs as the dancers pivoted from one side to the other; fragments of horses, high-stepping along gold-painted scrolled plaster mouldings. Women here and there in the festooned recesses. Some with cruel heels. Felt hats. Others more turn-of-the-century feminine, but with that wildness in their eyes that drives Lydia crazy.

The waitress leans over and says something to her.

"Yes"

Lydia replies, holding trance-like onto the thread (determined to stay elated). The horses were mostly white. Conjuring up mare-goddesses in the minds of some in the audience; or else, green wild dreams. The way they always walked switching their tails. Past her grandmother's house near the railway tracks. The village lesbian proudly mounted on one. As a child the attraction so strong, Lydia was terrified to approach her.

The walking woman moves farther up The Main. Now well beyond the swinging green-chipped door. Trying not to think of the down on her lover's lips. Towards the area of railyards and vast depots (desperate people are immune to danger). But is that guy still behind her? Lydia shivers violently. Her mind shattering (protectively) into small views of the street (ignoring the studio door). Shops with barrelsful of hard pink and green candy. Magazine stands. Hardware goods on slanted wood floors. Lunch counters exuding the smell of hamburger. With those damn old-fashioned headphones, Cello would never hear a footfall on the stairs. Sitting there, impeccable in loose shirt, large shoes, jodhpur pants (under which Lydia can't resist imagining the kind of panties and pubic hair). Her lips still mocking in the microphone.

(It's true their attitude caused resentment.)

"Alors mes belles, le mot de passe est *vivre*. Ne perdez pas votre temps avec les imbéciles."

The scraping of a chair—only the waitress pointedly tidying up around the few remaining stragglers. Lydia grasps more eagerly at the thread: the truth being she can only face her empty room if totally elated. She smiles, even politer. Hoping the man following the woman up The Main could have stopped and is hiding behind a column. As opposed to going up the radio station stairs. The scrape of a chair—probably Cello, tidying up as the tango draws out its last plaintive notes. Hurrying, no doubt, to meet someone at the women's bar. Lydia focuses on the music. In the tango, the dance must entirely take possession of the couple. But was there someone climbing up the radio station stairs? C. would certainly hear (having removed the headphones). She could hear every rustle in the desert. Crouched down in the fuchsia very rapid dusk, the horizontal light putting in relief the ample hair on her arm, looking for traces of reptiles or predators. Or waiting for her friend the large-eyed mule deer. Mostly she went alone. But (Lydia thought, gluttonously), there is nothing like making love to a woman on the sand. The few salty grains in the mouth. Trying to keep the faint salt stream from wasting on the ground. Attached to catch every drop, slow as the valve starts to flutter, then deluge—

Lydia's eyes close in pleasure. As the last strains of the last tango float out, towards the starry sky. She has the evening's repertoire in her head. The one, *Malena*, about the girl who put her whole heart into every line she sang (the only way you can); about women too angry now to love (actually it's men who are angry in this kind of music); about cigarettes, moonlit patios, empty cafés, high-heeled boots with knives. *En l'attendant j'ai bu indéfatigablement:* the waitress puts a firm yet friendly hand on Lydia's shoulder.

The guy walks up the stairs and into the ante-room.

C. leans over and takes something gleaming from her boot.

Kicking back her chair, with an impatient flick of her foot. Like Lydia, now, in the bar.

Nous autres, nous continuerons à vivre.

Lunging.


Lydia steps (a zigzag, to the air of a tango) into the night.

ACKNOWLEDGEMENTS

The author wishes to thank the Canada Council, le
Ministère de la Culture, and the Ontario Arts Council for
financial assistance.

Some of this work has appeared in *West Coast Line,*
*The Moosehead Anthology, Arcade, The Massachusetts*
*Review, The American Voice,* and, in earlier versions, in
the following anthologies: *Hard Times,* ed., Beverley
Daurio, Mercury Press, Stratford; *Resurgent,* eds., Camille
Norton and Lou Robinson, University of Illinois Press,
Urbana; *Serious Hysterics,* ed., Alison Fell, Serpent's Tail,
London (England).

I wish to thank, especially, Erin Mouré for faith,
hope and (many) charitable readings.

Thanks also to Lynn Lapointe and Martha Fleming.
The backdrop of the set for the performance piece
in Chapter 14 ("Night Music") is in homage to, and par-
tially inspired by their marvellous installation, *La Donna*
*Delinquenta.* Their work, as well as that of several other
Montréal women artists, has informed this book's sense of

women in urban space. Thanks to Nell Tenhaaf and Cheryl Sourkes. Many thanks to Bruce Russell, and also to Trevor Boddy for advice on architectural terminology. Thanks to Cristina Trowbridge.

*First We Take Manhattan,* © 1988, Leonard Cohen, Strange Music Inc. Used by permission.

The italicized lines on page 18 are from Kathy Acker's novel *Great Expectations,* New York: Grove Press, 1983.

Editors for the Press: Frank Davey and Susan Swan

Printed in Canada

COACH HOUSE PRESS

50 Prince Arthur Avenue

Suite 107

Toronto, Canada

M5R 1B5